The Scar

ZONDERVAN HEARTH BOOKS

Available from your Christian Bookseller

A HEARTH ROMANCE

The Scar

Sallie Lee Bell

ZONDERVAN
PUBLISHING HOUSE

OF THE ZONDERVAN CORPORATION | GRAND RAPIDS, MICHIGAN 49506

THE SCAR

Copyright © 1965 by Zondervan Publishing House
Grand Rapids, Michigan

First Zondervan Books edition 1974
Seventh printing 1979
ISBN 0-310-21032-1

Library of Congress Catalog Card Number 64-8836

Printed in the United States of America

CHAPTER 1

Beth Harris sat at the piano and let her fingers run idly over the keys. Her thoughts were not on what she was playing, for she was thinking of what had happened yesterday. She had been nominated as a candidate for Beauty Queen of the campus and her heart beat with joy as she remembered that exciting moment. She had not sought the nomination, for she knew that her mother had hoped that she wouldn't consent to having her name posted. It seemed such a flagrant attempt to display her beauty and her mother feared that it might create the vanity that she had tried to keep from gaining possession of Beth.

However, when Beth had been nominated, she didn't refuse to let her name be posted. It was an honor that she couldn't resist or refuse to accept.

Beth was not only beautiful, but she possessed a talent for music that enabled her to play the piano and any other instrument she tried to master. She had a lovely voice that was above average, clear and mellow, and which was able to reach the high notes of the scale with no apparent effort.

A smile flitted across her face as her thoughts reverted to the events of yesterday. Presently she began to play a melody that she loved, a difficult but beautiful number. Her fingers flew over the keys as she enjoyed the beauty of the composition. When that was finished, she began to play an old love song that her mother had taught her when she was a little child.

Her mother tiptoed to the door and stood there watching her and her heart throbbed with pride as she looked upon her only child. Beth's hair fell in soft golden waves to her shoulders and her blue eyes, shaded by the long curling lashes, were raised as she sang the words and felt the pathos of them — "I'll take you home again, Kathleen," her lovely voice rose forth softly.

How proud she was of this child of hers, her mother thought, as she watched the delicately molded face with features that were almost perfect. Yet her heart was heavy. Beth's beauty could be a snare to her and a hindrance instead of an asset. She knew that Beth was not protected from any temptation that Satan might throw across her path, for she had never put her trust in the Lord and His protection.

As Beth finished the song, she turned to her mother, for she had felt her presence there in the doorway.

"That was beautiful," her mother remarked as she gave Beth a smile.

"Thanks, Mommy," Beth replied as she returned the smile. "I love that old song because you taught it to me, but it always makes me feel sad when I know that Kathleen never got to see the land she loved. That's the way it is with so many things in life. They never turn out the way they should."

"Why so pessimistic?" her mother inquired. "Has something happened to upset you?"

"No. I was just talking. I'm as happy as can be. Why shouldn't I be?"

"That's the way I want you to be always," her mother said as she approached and placed a kiss on the top of Beth's head. "Now sing my favorite gospel song."

"Don't you ever get tired of that old song?" Beth asked resignedly.

"No, because it's just what I feel," her mother replied.

Obediently Beth's fingers ran lightly over an introduction, then her sweet voice rang out in the words, "I'd Rather Have Jesus."

She was artist enough to put her whole soul into the

lovely song and as her mother listened, tears came into her eyes.

"Thank you, honey," she said. She put her arm around Beth and bent down and kissed her on her cheek. "If you could only sing those words and really mean what they say, I'd be the happiest person in the world. Why can't you see how wonderful your life would be if you could sing those words from your heart?"

"Oh Mom, don't start that again," Beth remonstrated. "I don't feel like listening to a sermon now."

"I'm not preaching, only wishing," her mother said sadly. "You know that I dedicated you to the Lord before you were born and I prayed that you would give your heart and your life to the Lord and serve Him and find joy in service."

"Yes, Mommy," Beth replied resignedly. "You've told me that so many times before. I'm sorry that I can't be what you want me to be when it comes to religion, but I do try to please you in every other way. Why not let me live my life the way I want to? I'm not a bad girl. You know that."

"I know, honey. You give me joy in every way but in the one thing that I want for you more than anything else."

"Please, Mom! Give me time. I'm young and I want to get some fun out of life before I settle down to living the kind of life you want me to live. There's plenty of time for me to live for the Lord, but let me live for myself a little while longer."

"That's what frightens me, Beth, darling," her mother replied. "None of us knows how long we will be allowed to live and if the Lord should see fit to cut your life short, then where would you be? Lost in an eternity without God."

"Oh, Mother! You're spoiling a perfectly lovely day," Beth said impatiently. "I've got such a lot to live for right now. I didn't tell you what happened yesterday. I wanted to wait and surprise you if I got what I think

9

I'll get. I was nominated as one of the beauty queens of the campus."

"That's wonderful," her mother said and gave her a smile, but the smile soon vanished and she looked serious. "I'm sorry you entered the contest. You know how I feel about those contests. They have ruined many a young person. It can make a girl vain and selfish and when she doesn't get what she hopes for, she is bitter and feels defeated for the rest of her life."

"I didn't enter the contest," Beth said defensively. "They put my name in without even asking my consent. Naturally, I hope I'll win."

"And if you don't win, what then? You'll be disappointed, and I don't want you to feel bitter."

"If I don't win, I'll know that some conniving person will control that contest and put someone else over. I'll just laugh at them for being so blind and stupid," she said playfully and gave her mother a kiss. "Don't worry about me, Mommy dear, I won't be disappointed. I'll just know how stupid the ones were who voted me down. I know I'm pretty, but since, as you've told me, I didn't make myself pretty, I have nothing to boast about." She smiled roguishly at her mother.

"That's true," her mother said seriously. "Since you had nothing to do about being so lovely, you should never be vain about it, but just thankful to God who made you what you are."

"Stop! Stop!" Beth cried and threw up her hands. "No more of that now. I can't stand anymore. Let's go out to the kitchen and stir up a batch of cookies. I feel like cooking."

They went arm and arm into the kitchen and were soon busy with the cookies. Mr. Harris came in just as they were taking the first batch from the oven.

"My! That smells good!" he exclaimed. "How about giving me a sample?"

He kissed his wife and Beth, and Beth broke off a piece from a cookie and put it in his mouth.

"If you say it's super, you may have the rest of it,"

10

she said and waited with a smile while he disposed of the morsel.

"Super," he ejaculated, and she laughingly gave him the rest.

Her father was an extremely young-looking man, tall and slender and quite good-looking. Beth had inherited his features. His wife was small and dark, with a sweet face that was not beautiful, but which glowed with a light from within that made her very attractive. They had been Christians and sweethearts since they were in high school together.

"You go on and let Dad give you all the news which I know you're dying to hear and I'll clean up here," Beth told her mother as she pushed her toward the door.

As they left, she turned to her work with a song upon her lips, a lilting melody that expressed the joy that was bubbling up within her. She was thinking of the balloting that would take place on Monday and of the thrill that would be hers if she were crowned queen of the campus at the game during homecoming week. If she wasn't elected, she shrugged, she'd just sit on the sidelines and try not to be too disappointed.

When her parents reached their room and Mr. Harris prepared to clean up, he saw the serious expression on his wife's face.

"What's wrong, honey?" he asked tenderly, putting an arm around her and kissing her.

"Did I say there was anything wrong?" she parried as she looked up at him and stroked his cheek.

"You don't have to say. I can tell. Has Beth been up to something?"

Though Beth had never given them a moment's worry, he knew that she was reaching the age when temptation might change the picture.

"No," she said hesitantly, "but something has happened that makes me a little worried."

"Out with it. Let's have it and get it over with, so that I can put her across my knee and give her the paddling that she hasn't needed for a long time."

His wife smiled rather feebly. "She hasn't done anything that would need such drastic measures. The school put her name up for election as beauty queen of the campus."

"Why, that's wonderful!" he exclaimed. "Of course she'll win. She's the prettiest little thing in that school."

"But I don't want her to be elected," his wife argued. "I know what a snare it can be, since she hasn't given her life to the Lord. I know what it can do her; what it has done for others. I want Beth to be as beautiful within as she is without. I don't want her beauty to be a snare, but an asset. It can be a snare if she refuses to give her life to the Lord."

"Don't look on the dark side," her husband advised. "Let's just hope that our prayers will be answered and that she'll be the most beautiful little Christian this town has ever seen."

He gave her a smile and another light kiss and went into the bathroom to freshen up.

His wife's face was still serious as he finally came out and they went downstairs together.

CHAPTER 2

Beth had just finished cleaning up the kitchen when the telephone rang. It was her friend Laurie reminding her to come over to the tennis court and make a foursome for their game.

The state college was not far from where Beth lived. There were several courts available to the students, but they were always in demand on afternoons and Saturdays, and students had to engage them for a short time for their games. Beth had forgotten that her group had engaged it for a time this afternoon.

She told her mother about the call and then hastened to change her dress. When she went out with her racket over her shoulder, her eyes were sparkling.

"She's the loveliest little angel that ever walked this earth," her father remarked as they watched her go.

"Isn't that an exaggeration and aren't you getting things just a little mixed?" his wife asked with a smile. "She's not an angel and never will be one, as you well know. Sometimes she doesn't in the least resemble one when she gets angry and lets her temper fly. I wish that her soul was as beautiful as her body is." A sigh escaped her.

"Don't worry, honey," he advised. "She'll come around to our way of believing. Just give her time. We'll just keep on praying and believing."

"I shall do that, but sometimes I get a little impatient to see my prayer answered."

"Where's your faith?" he asked, as he put an arm around her and gave her a gentle shake.

13

Beth went on her way blithely, ignorant of what was taking place between her parents as they watched her. She was thinking of the game, and hoping that she could win this set between Gary and herself, against Laurie and Bob.

Gary Donovan was a quiet, studious fellow who had been in love with Beth since they were small children. He was not handsome, yet there was a certain attraction in his strong face with the dark expressive eyes and the firm mouth. He would smile occasionally with a smile that was so attractive that it made him seem actually handsome.

Beth thought of him as she tripped gaily toward the courts. Good old Gary. How faithful he had been and how persistent in his effort to win her love, even before they were old enough to think seriously of love. She remembered with a smile, how her slightest harsh word could put the shadows in those childish eyes when they played together. She also remembered that often she had purposely been cross with him just so she could see that little face become clouded with pain. Then she would ask for his forgiveness and see that rare smile light up his face and transform it.

When she grew older and realized her beauty, and when other boys were attracted by her beauty, she seemed to possess a fiendish delight in showing other boys an exaggerated delight in their attentions. Gary never rebuked her for this and she would never have tolerated it if he had, but that dark cloud would drift across his face and into his eyes and he would slip off to loneliness, refusing to retaliate by showing some other girl his attention. She was the one girl in the world for him and he made no secret of it. Sometimes she felt guilty because she hurt him so often, but she just couldn't keep from it. It gave her a mean little feeling of elation to know that she had such power over him.

When Gary entered college, she felt a sense of loss, for he was so intent upon his studies that he had very little time for her or anyone else. He was majoring in languages and hoped to be a college professor. Beth was disappointed, for she had grown so used to his adulation. However, she realized that he had grown older and wiser and that he was now more able to control his feelings. Though he loved her and knew that she was the only girl in the world for him, he had no hope of winning her. She was so surrounded by admirers, many of them boys of wealth and position, that he felt he could never win her for himself.

They were still close friends, and she could occasionally get a glimpse in his eyes of the light that had always been there when he looked at her in the past. However, he never presumed upon her friendship.

He had asked her to be his partner in the games they were to play this afternoon, but she had forgotten it during the excitement over the nomination of the beauty queen candidates.

"Hurry up, Queenie," Bob called to her as she neared the court. "You're delaying the game."

"You're a little premature with that title, don't you think?" Beth asked as she joined them. "Don't put the crown on my head until I'm elected to wear it."

"You will be, honey," Laurie affirmed. "You know those others don't have a chance. I can't even be jealous because I wasn't nominated. I'd only be disappointed when the election was over and I had lost to you."

"You should have been nominated," Beth told her. "I think you're adorable," and she put an arm around her chum and gave her a hug.

Gary said nothing, but his eyes were fastened upon her with a rapt gaze.

"How about it, fellow?" Bob asked, poking him with his racket. "Can't you at least tell the queen that she has your vote?"

"She knows that without my telling her," Gary answered quietly.

"Oh, I see," Bob remarked with a grin. "You've got a secret code all worked out between you."

15

"We've had that ever since I can remember," Gary retorted with one of his rare smiles, while his eyes rested upon Beth.

"Then there's no hope for the rest of us," Bob said and uttered an exaggerated sigh.

"You're wrong," Gary told him while the smile faded and his eyes became serious. "The field's open and may the best man win. I used to think it was closed, but I've learned better. Wisdom sometimes comes slowly, but it finally sinks in."

Beth gave him a surprised look. She felt hurt by his remark. For the first time she felt that he had not only grown up, but that he had grown away from her. There was a wall between them and the old relation was gone forever. Strangely, some of the joy faded and the song in her heart was silenced.

"Come on, let's play," Laurie urged. "Time is passing and we'll have to give up the court before we get started."

Beth played the game with her usual spirit and her flair for making wild and spectacular plays, while Gary played doggedly and skillfully. They won the set.

"Boy! Did we get blitzed!" Bob cried. "I'm all out of breath trying to hit those vanishing balls."

They sat down for awhile to rest and then began another set. When they finally had to relinquish the court to another foursome, they walked together for a time, then Bob and Laurie left while Beth and Gary walked toward her home.

They were silent for a time, for he was not given to idle chatter, and Beth was trying to get used to his new mood. He had seemed to be more formal and distant during the last semester, but it had never been quite as evident as it was today.

"That was the best game we've had for a long time," she remarked, trying to start a conversation. "In fact, it's the first one I've had with you for ages."

"Someone was always ahead of me," he replied.

"There needn't have been," she said reproachfully.

"You know I always like to play with you."

She was more hurt then ever by his seeming coldness. Suddenly she felt that she could no longer take him for granted. She had never realized that he was a man now, almost twenty, and that he was taking life more seriously. She had still thought of him as a boy older than she, but playing down to her level because he worshiped her so.

"I'm glad you do," he said slowly, "but I know there are others who would also like to play with you and I don't want to monopolize you."

"How considerate of you!" she flashed sarcastically, hurt and angry at his coldness and sudden indifference.

"Not considerate, just being sensible," he corrected. "I know that I can't expect to keep you in a corner away from all the others who swarm around you, so why try? I'm grateful for what I can have and I'll not cry for something that is out of my reach."

"What do you mean by that?" she asked.

"Let's forget it, shall we? You played magnificently today and it gave me a thrill to be playing as your partner. You really won the games."

"Thanks, though that's not true," she replied coldly.

They had reached her home and she asked if he would come in.

"We'd be glad to have you stay for dinner," she said. "It's been a long time since you've taken a meal with us. Mother said the other day that she missed you. Remember how you always used to manage to hang around near mealtime so that you'd be invited to eat with us?"

She smiled, but there was no answering smile from him.

"I remember with shame what a little moocher I was, but it was just to be near you that much longer. Children can be such foolish little monsters. Thank you for inviting me, but I've got to get back to those books. I'm getting Spanish and French and Latin so muddled

17

that I don't know which is which. It's been good to be with you again."

"Aren't you going to wish me good luck in the voting?" she asked as he was turning away.

He turned back and looked into her deep blue eyes. There was a light in his that she had never seen before. It was the light of a man who loved a girl, not of a litle boy who had adored her and had hung upon her favor.

"I don't know if I should. For if I did, I wouldn't be telling the truth," he said soberly. "You're beautiful enough and popular enough to win without a doubt, but if you do win, you'll be farther away from me than ever."

He turned and left her abruptly after a murmured goodby. She stood looking after him while her heart stirred strangely. In all the years that he had been her abject slave, she had never felt as lonely and deserted as she did at this moment.

There was pain in her heart. All the joy and excitement over the coming election vanished, leaving only longing for something which she had taken for granted all these years. If he still cared, he was seemingly determined not to let it control him any longer. She felt that she had lost something more precious than being crowned queen or having a host of other admirers at her feet. If she couldn't see that adoring light in his cycs on that great day; if she should be elected, the admiration and attention of all the others who had been charmed by her beauty and personality would mean so little.

As she climbed the steps and went inside, there was no smile upon her lips and the sparkle in her eyes had vanished.

CHAPTER 3

Beth was in a subdued spirit as she sat at the table that evening. Her mother noticed it and she remarked about it as they began the meal.

"Did you have a good game, dear?" she asked.

"Yes, I did. We beat them two sets," Beth told her. "I never played better and even Bob remarked about it."

"What did Gary say?" her father asked with a twinkle in his eye.

Both he and his wife had been aware of Gary's adoration of Beth ever since they were small children. They had lived next door to each other until a short time ago.

"He didn't say anything, as usual," Beth replied, rather petulantly.

"The strong, silent type are usually the most sincere and more worthwhile than the gushy, talkative type," her father remarked.

"That may be true," Beth admitted, "but a person likes a little less silence sometimes."

"You and Gary didn't quarrel, did you?" her mother asked anxiously.

She liked Gary because he was a Christian and she hoped that one day Beth would return his love and marry him.

"No, we couldn't do that," Beth told her. "He wouldn't quarrel even if I wanted to. But he's so wrapped up in that career of his that he has no time for a little fun. I'd hate to be tied to a person like that for the rest of my life. I'd have to do all the talking and it should be a fifty-fifty affair."

"You could carry on your part and then some," her

father remarked with a little laugh. "You've had plenty of practice."

"Shame on you, Daddy," Beth said with an exaggerated pout. "I never try to do more talking than the occasion demands."

He patted her hand while he gave her a tender smile. "I'm satisfied with you, honey, and I love to hear you talk."

Beth was provoked with herself for having that disappointed feeling about Gary, but he hadn't paid her a compliment in ever so long and he didn't say one word about her nomination as one of the campus queens until she had almost forced him to. He used to worry her by his little words of endearment that were uttered so ungrammatically, but which came from his heart. She wondered if he were becoming interested in someone else, because he was tired of her domineering spirit and her taking him for granted. Though it was a foolish fear, she became uneasy. What had made him crawl into this shell of silence and indifference, if it wasn't some other girl who treated him better than she had? She was sorry that she had treated him so, but perhaps it was too late to be sorry. When they were children, he hadn't seemed to mind. If she hurt him, he would go away and pout for a little while, but he would return with his little boy eagerness to please her and play whatever game she insisted upon playing. She should have known that, now that he was no longer a child, he wouldn't tolerate such treatment.

When Sunday came, she went dutifully to church with her parents, but her mind was not on the sermon. It should have made her realize more forcibly than ever, that she was a lost soul, for the preacher was a consecrated person who gave out the truth.

During the sermon, Mrs. Harris prayed and hoped that Beth would be stirred to realize her lost condition, but as she stole a glance at Beth, she realized that she wasn't listening.

Beth scanned the congregation for a sight of Gary.

She hoped that he wouldn't be sitting beside some other girl. In the old days he had often slipped in to sit beside her. She finally saw him across the aisle. Her heart seemed suddenly lighter, but when the service was over, he left without even looking in her direction, though she knew that he must have seen her where she always sat.

On the way home her father mentioned the sermon.

"I never heard a more convincing message," he remarked. "I don't see how anyone could sit there and not be convicted of his lost condition."

"It was one of the best messages I've heard in a long time," his wife observed. "Wasn't it inspiring, the way he brought in the return of the Lord? But it's frightening to think of those who won't be ready when He comes. What did you think of it, dear?" she asked Beth.

"I'm afraid I wasn't listening," Beth admitted. "I was thinking of that test I'm having tomorrow."

She was also thinking of the election of the campus queen and wondering what her dress should be like, if she won.

Monday dawned bright and sunny and Beth took it as an omen that she would win the election.

"Wish me victory, Mommy," she said as she kissed her mother before she left.

"I always pray for the best in life for you dear," her mother replied seriously. "If it's best for you to win, I know you will, but if the Lord doesn't want you to win, don't be too disappointed."

"That's not a very enthusiastic wish," Beth remarked, disappointed and a little bit afraid at the mention of the Lord's name. She knew His power, even if she didn't accept His salvation, for her mother had instilled the knowledge of the Lord and His Word into her from the time she was old enough to understand. She hoped with all her heart that God would let her win. If He didn't she knew that she would be terribly disappointed.

Beth tried not to show her nervousness as time came for the ballots to be cast, but it was difficult and she could scarcely wait until the vote was counted and the winner announced. When the result was announced and Beth's name won, a cheer went up from the assembled students.

Laurie was the first one among the many who came to congratulate her. She gave Beth a hug and a kiss.

"I knew you'd win," she said. "I did a lot of lobbying to get votes for you."

"She didn't need your help," said one of the girls standing near. "She'd have won without your help. We love you, Beth, and we were all pulling for you."

By the time Beth had been kissed by the girls and had shaken the hands of countless boys, she was exhausted from excitement and the strain. Her face felt numb from her fixed smile and she was glad when all of them had left.

She realized that Gary hadn't been among her well-wishers. Her heart sank and much of the thrill of her victory left her. Why hadn't he at least been there to congratulate her? For old times' sake, he could at least have wished her well.

As she walked toward the gate of the campus, she saw him there waiting. He joined her as she approached. There was a smile upon his face, one of his rare smiles, and her heart suddenly felt light again.

"Is it too late to pay homage to the queen?" he asked as he walked beside her.

"Do you have to be sarcastic?" she replied tartly. It wasn't what she had hoped to hear.

"I wasn't being sarcastic," he said as the smile faded. "There were so many crowding around you that I would have felt silly trying to get a word in edgewise. I waited here, hoping that my congratulations wouldn't be too superfluous after all the others you had heard."

"You ought to know that what you say could never be that," she said with a reproachful glance.

"But I didn't know," he repeated. "You've been sur-

22

rounded by so many since we came here that I thought perhaps you had forgotten or else outgrown the past. I didn't want to intrude."

"Why do you keep on saying you don't want to intrude?" she asked. "As if I ever could forget the past or outgrow it. You've been such a part of my life for so long that it would be like tearing out a part of it not to have you around."

"That's what I thought," he said gravely. "You've just been used to having me around. I've been as someone whom you would count on, whom you could abuse or fall back on when there was no one else around to claim your attention."

"How can you say that!" she exclaimed angrily. "I've never acted that way at all," but she knew that she wasn't telling the truth, for that was the way she had treated him. "I'm sorry if you feel that way," she added contritely.

"Then may I add my congratulations?" he asked. "I knew you would win and so did practically everyone else. I hope that your victory will bring you joy and that it won't prove a snare to you in any way."

"Why should it prove to be a snare?" she asked.

"If I say more, you'll say I'm preaching and I've been ordered long ago not to do any more of that. But sometimes our greatest success brings sorrow instead of joy and on the contrary, our greatest disappointments prove to be God's appointments."

"Now you're talking like Mother," she said. "I heard a sermon on that subject the day I was nominated as one of the candidates."

"Then I dare not give you another," he replied and began to talk of other things.

When they reached her home, they stood and talked for a few moments.

"Believe me, little Beth," he said tenderly, "I shall always wish for you the best that life can hold, the best in happiness and contentment and success in everything you undertake."

"You talk as if you'll never see me again," she said with a nervous little laugh.

"I'll be seeing you often again, I hope, but it may be from a distance, for the queen will be surrounded by her court and her admirers and there may be no room near her throne."

"If there isn't any room for you, it'll be your own fault," she told him. "Only those who really care will want to be there."

"That's not usually true with royalty," he argued. "The ones who care are usually pushed into the background by the ones seeking favor from the throne."

"Stop speaking in riddles," she advised. "If you're not there in the front ranks, I shall know that it is because you no longer care, that you have forgotten the old days."

"I could never forget them," he said gravely. "'Of all the pictures hung on memories' walls'," he quoted, "the pictures of that past will never fade out. Good-by. I know you're tired and need rest. I shall be there at the crowning of the queen."

CHAPTER 4

When Beth entered the house, her heart was singing and her spirits soared. It was not caused by her winning the election. It was Gary's tender voice when he spoke of the past. If he hadn't forgotten — but how could he, when it wasn't so far distant? Then he hadn't lost the feeling he had had for her. Hope grew within her. Even though she had the attention of so many others, she still longed to keep Gary in her number of admirers. She realized that he knew this was just what she wanted and perhaps he thought that this was the only reason she had wanted to continue their relationship. She also realized that he had too much pride to let that status continue, now that he was grown and could look at life more clearly. Worship of her could not take first place in his life as it had done when there were no responsibilities in that life.

Her mother was waiting for her when she came in and she knew by the expression upon Beth's face that she had won.

"I don't have to ask if you won," she remarked with a tender smile as Beth came in. "I can see victory in your face."

Beth gave her a kiss and a hug.

"You've got mighty keen eyes," she said. "Yes, I won by an overwhelming majority, as they would say in a political campaign. Everyone was lovely to me, even the girls who were running against me. Of course they'll be my maids."

"I'm glad for you, honey, if it makes you happy.

25

And I'm glad that everyone was so nice to you. It was mighty sweet for the other girls to congratulate you and wish you well."

"You're just a little sorry that I won, aren't you?" Beth asked anxiously.

"Let's not talk about that now," her mother replied. "I want you to enjoy what you've won and I pray that it won't bring any regrets."

"How can it, Mommy? I'll do everything I can to let it make me more deserving of it. Now I'll have to think about the dress I shall wear when they crown me and I'll have to have a new dress for the big celebration after the game."

"We'll have time to think about that," her mother told her. "I'll have to get into the kitchen now and start supper. We'll talk that over tonight."

She was thinking of the expense. They lived on a rather limited budget. She wanted Beth to have the best that she could afford. She sewed beautifully and she thought she could make the dress. When they discussed it that evening, Beth was sure that her mother could make something that she would be proud to wear.

The day of the game was bright and warm and the entire school was excited. The queen and her court arrived amidst the blare of trumpets and the coronation march by the college band. Between halves Beth was crowned with a colorful ceremony while her maids were grouped about her, young and lovely in their becoming dresses. Beth wore white and many remarked, as the sun shone down upon her golden hair, making it resemble a halo of gold under the glittering crown, that she was the loveliest queen that had ever been crowned there.

Her father and mother were in reserved seats near the queen and her court and they couldn't help but be proud and happy as they watched their child receiving such an ovation.

The last half of the game was tinged with the keenest

26

excitement. The score was tied until, at the very end, by a field goal, Clinton won amid the shouts and jubilant screams of the Clinton fans.

Beth ate a hurried meal when she reached home. She was too excited to eat much and after she finished, she slipped out of the house dress she had on and began to prepare for the celebration that evening.

She had looked for Gary at the game, but she couldn't find him. She wondered if he were there. She hoped that he was, for she wanted him, more than anyone else, to see her in her royal robes. Her eyes had glowed with a pleased light as she surveyed herself in the mirror before she left for the stadium. She saw without any feeling of vanity how beautiful she was. How she hoped he had seen her.

When she reached the gymnasium where the celebration was to be held, many had already arrived and there was a buzz of conversation mingled with laughter. When she entered with her escort, however, every eye was focused on her and there were murmured comments about her loveliness. Her dress was pale blue, with little spangles bordering the curve of the neck.

The members of the team, dressed in formal attire, looked quite different from the way they had looked on the field in the dust of scrimmage, with their enormous shoulder pads and protecting helmets.

A few minutes after Beth arrived, Harold Brandon, the hero of the evening, the outstanding player of the season and the one who had made the winning field goal, came to her and asked her if he might have the first dance. She was surprised and pleased, but she told him that she would have to dance with her escort first.

"Even a hero must obey the queen's request," he answered with a smile. "I'll be waiting for you for the next dance."

Beth had not told her mother that there would be dancing and her mother had not even thought to ask. She had forgotten that in this era, few gatherings were considered a success if there was not dancing. Beth had

27

learned to dance when she was in high school, something else that she had not told her mother. Laurie had insisted upon teaching her.

"If you don't dance when you get to college, you surely will be a wall flower," Laurie had told her. "You'll be the only one who has to sit on the side lines because you don't know how to dance. Then what will you feel like?"

Tonight she was glad that she knew how to dance, that she had kept in practice in the gymnasium, dancing with the girls. Her partner, Fred Stevens, looked rather glum when they began to dance. He heard what Harold had said.

"Your whole evening will be taken up with that guy," he remarked as they glided across the floor. "He thinks all he has to do is to look at a girl and she'll fall over in a faint."

"Then I'm glad that he never looked at me before," Beth replied with a smile. "I surely wouldn't want to be that silly."

"You sure have got 'em all beat here tonight," he remarked, giving her an admiring glance. "There are a lot of good lookers here, but they can't come up to you."

"Thank you," she said demurely.

She was glad when the dance was over and Fred led her over to one side to wait for the next dance. Fred wasn't too entertaining and she wondered how she had consented to let him bring her here tonight. She could have put him off with an excuse for she knew that others would ask her to let them bring her.

"I'll see you again, if that fellow gives me a chance," he said as he left her.

"Funny, I never noticed you before," Harold remarked as they began to dance.

"Why should a hero look at a humble junior?" she asked.

"I must have been blind as well as stupid. I'll say

28

with the screen idols, 'Where have you been all my life?'"

"Right under your nose, sir," she said roguishly. "I've clapped until my hands were sore and screamed myself hoarse over you time after time during a ball game."

"And all that time I didn't know you were there," he exclaimed. "What I've missed all these years! And to think that this is my last year. I shall hate to leave you here to the wolves on the campus."

"I'm sure you'll survive the loss," she replied.

"Atta boy!" he said and laughed. "You know how to kick back the answers. Why is it that so many pretty girls are so dumb?"

"And why is it that so many of you heroes on the field are so arrogant and opinionated?" she flashed back.

"Wow! That was a keen one! Honestly, if I've been that bad, I never meant to be. I'm sorry and regret that I never met you before."

"Oh, you've met me before, but I didn't register," she said. "And forgive me if I've been rude. I didn't mean to be."

"I must have been blind if you didn't register. Believe me, you do now. May I have a date with you soon — very soon?"

"I'll think about it," she conceded.

When the dance ended he thanked her for a delightful time.

"I'll be back again, if I may have another dance," he whispered as he left her.

"Perhaps," she replied.

She searched the room for a glimpse of Gary, but she didn't see him. She felt sure he would be there for a little while at least, for this celebration was only for the upper classes and she knew that he would feel obligated to come.

He had been there for a little while before the dancing had begun. He congratulated Harold upon his victory in the game and he saw Beth when she came in. His eyes lingered long upon her glowing face, then he had seen her begin the dance with Fred and he had left. It hurt him to see Beth dancing. He knew how her mother felt about this and he wondered if she was aware that Beth knew how to dance. He wondered what would happen to her life after this. He felt that she was farther from him than ever. In another year he would be out and on his own, and she would be left to the attentions of others who were better able to take care of a wife than he ever would be. He would be making the salary of a teacher when he had finished graduate school, while many of these boys who hovered about Beth were from wealthy families and could give her everything.

If she had loved him enough, he might have been able to lead her to the Lord, but he felt that she had never really loved him. She had loved herself and her power over him, and had gloried in his abject slavery to his love for her.

His heart was heavy, for he felt that the dream of his life had come to a sad awakening. She wasn't for him, yet she would always be the one girl for him. The love of a lifetime couldn't be easily forgotten or overcome. It had made a part of his life for too long.

Loneliness and heartache assailed him as he made his way home and sat down to a couple of hours of study. However, it was hard to keep his mind upon it and to keep from thinking of Beth enjoying the admiration of her beauty and dancing her way out of his life.

CHAPTER 5

Beth was flattered by the attention that Harold Brandon paid her. As he had admitted with regret, he had never particularly noticed her before. Now he was with her on every occasion.

He had paid attention to many others before, but Gary noticed that these girls were either wealthy or high on the social scale. He wondered how long his attentions to Beth would last. He feared that if Beth began to care for Harold she would be let down and hurt.

He knew that this boy, who had personality as well as looks, and who was now a hero because of his ball playing, was not only not a Christian, but also the kind of boy to whom Beth should not give her heart. He kept out of trouble because he knew he couldn't afford to lose his scholarship which was given because of his skill as a football player. He lived, however, in danger of being expelled, if his exploits were discovered.

Beth, since she had become the queen, was someone new, a new attraction, and Gary knew that Harold had the power and the personality to win her interest. He wanted to add Beth to his list of conquests.

Beth won the envy of some of the girls and the animosity of others who had been his dates before he had begun to notice her. She noticed the coolness of some of the girls, and was sorry to lose their friendship, but she was too much interested in Harold to let it worry her.

She seldom saw Gary except in passing to and from

classes. They did walk to her home together occasionally when they were free from classes at the same time.

"You're almost a stranger these days," she remarked on one of these afternoons. "I never have a chance to even talk to you anymore."

"You never give me the opportunity," he replied. "Your time is too taken up with the hero of the campus."

"Now that isn't a very nice remark," she stated. "It doesn't sound like you. It sounds like some of those jealous girls who used to go with Harold.

"I'm not jealous, if that's what you're hinting," he said solemnly. "But I am worried because that boy is paying you so much attention. He's deprived you of the attentions of other boys who are much more worthy of you than he is."

"What do you mean by that?" she asked tartly. "What are you trying to tell me about Harold? I like him and I like to be with him. He's made it quite plain that he likes me a lot. What do you have against him?"

"Nothing that I would be willing to tell you, but I repeat that he's not the kind of boy you should be interested in. He's going with you because of your recent election. When the novelty wears off, he'll drop you like he has the other girls he used to go with. I don't want you to be hurt, Beth."

"You needn't worry about me," she said loftily. "I'm able to take care of myself. A boy has a right to change his mind. If he found me more attractive than those others, why is that so wrong?"

"Have you noticed how often he's changed his mind?" he persisted. "First it was that pretty girl who came here from Western. He gave her the grand rush until he learned that Cynthia belonged to a high society crowd and that she could give him invitations to all the select social functions. Then he dropped the other girl. After that he met Nancy, who was quite wealthy, and he was invited to go with her on her father's yacht for a nice trip during mid-term vacation. She isn't pretty and I confess that she's not a very interesting person, but he dropped Cynthia and gave Nancy the grand rush until someone else came along who could give him all that Nancy could and more besides. Also she was quite pretty. You ought to know her, for she was one of your maids. And his last flame."

"And now she won't even speak to me," Beth remarked.

"Don't you see what is happening to you, Beth?" he asked tenderly. "You're just a passing fancy, and if you let yourself fall in love with him as some of those others have, you'll be hurt and I don't want to see you hurt."

"Are you trying to be a dog in the manger?" she asked. "You don't want me for yourself, yet you don't want anyone else to want me."

The words were out, but she was sorry she had uttered them, for she knew that they were rude and cheap and unworthy of her. But he had hurt her pride, and that pride had grown since the crowning of the queen. She was more sorry when she saw the hurt look in his eyes.

"No, I'm not trying to be a dog in the manger," he said slowly. "I've already told you that I didn't even want to think of you belonging to me. You've known how I've felt ever since I could remember, but I knew since I've become older, that you were not for me. I could never make you happy, so I left the field open to others who might be better able to make you happy. But I don't think Harold is one of them."

It was almost dark and the tree-shaded street was darker still. She looked up at him and there were tears in her eyes, though he didn't see them.

"I'm sorry if I hurt you, Gary," she said. "I didn't mean those rude, cheap words. But you've hurt me more than Harold ever could. I don't really care for him, but I do enjoy his company. There's no harm in that. Please forgive me."

She reached up and kissed him on his cheek. She had

done that many times in the past when they had had a childish quarrel, but it was the first time this had happened since they had grown older.

He put his arms around her and held her close while he kissed her tenderly, then clingingly upon her full red lips. She didn't resist the caress, but remained in the fold of his arms.

"You know what you mean to me," he said huskily, "but I'll never try to keep you from having the chance that you should have with someone who can make you happier than I ever could."

"And what could make me more happy than the love of someone who would always be kind and considerate and who loved me?" she asked as she remained in his arms.

"I would never be able to give you all that a beautiful woman would naturally want. A teacher's salary at best, is not sufficient to afford luxuries, and that seems to be what my life's work shall be. It's the one thing I've always wanted to do. Perhaps some day the Lord may call me to teach on some foreign field and if He does, I shall be willing to go, for I want to do His will above everything else."

"Don't you think that you could ever make me happy?" she asked.

She didn't know why she asked that question. Perhaps it was because she was just curious to know the answer, perhaps because his recent indifference had made him more important to her. She felt that part of the old life was slipping away from her and she didn't want to lose him. She didn't realize that she herself was being a dog in the manger, for she wanted to keep him while she accepted the attentions of others who were more glamorous and more attentive than he was now.

"Perhaps I might, if you were a Christian," he replied. "But since you're not, you're still more interested in things of the world than in spiritual things and my life would never be in harmony with yours. If you were a Christian, I'd spend my life trying to make you happy and we could be happy together. I've prayed earnestly that you would yield your heart to the Lord. Perhaps my prayer was a selfish one, but I did and still do long for your salvation. That's the only answer I can give you, Beth dear."

She withdrew from his arms. "I'm sorry you feel that way, but I can't change my life. Perhaps when I'm older and have had my fun, I may change, but not now. I don't want to change now. I want to be just what I am. I do try to be good, but that's all I can be now."

"Have you never thought that if you continue to feel that way, when you're older you'll feel that way even more strongly? You know, as well as I, that you can't come to God just when you make up your mind you'll come, but only when the Spirit leads you. And have you ever thought that you may never live to be old enough to want to give up those good times and give the Lord what's left of your misspent life?"

"No, and I don't want to think about that," she said stubbornly. "All I want to think of is what I'm doing now and the way I'm living now. Please don't make me think about dying, because I want to live."

"It's something we all have to face, if the Lord doesn't come before then. And only the ones who are ready to meet the Lord are the ones who're not afraid to think about dying. Death has no terror for them."

"I don't want to think about it," she repeated. "Please don't be angry with me, Gary. I need your friendship. Don't keep on avoiding me," she begged.

"You'll always have my friendship," he assured her. "But I think it best if I leave the way open for you to have your fun with the ones whom you think can give it to you. I just pray that you won't be hurt."

They parted at the corner. Beth was shaken and unhappy. She knew that she still cared for Gary as she had ever since they were children, though not in the way he cared for her. She felt lost without his presence, but she knew that she had no desire or plan to become a

Christian and to settle down to life as the wife of a schoolteacher. She wanted the attention of the many who were attracted by her beauty and just now Harold was the most interesting.

Gary walked home and his heart was heavy. He knew that Beth was getting farther and farther away from him and that he could do nothing about it. But he could still pray, and he was determined to keep on doing just that. He trusted that his faith would not waver, even though now it seemed quite weak.

CHAPTER 6

Beth was shaken and disappointed after that brief time under the trees. Her mother wondered what had kept her so late, for she usually came home much earlier. Beth told her that they had had a students' meeting and that she had walked home with Gary. Her mother was satisfied if she had been with Gary.

By the next day, however, she had recovered her spirits. She was determined not to heed the warning that Gary had tried to give her about Harold. She saw nothing wrong in accepting his attentions. She argued that she couldn't get rid of him if she had wanted to. If she tried, she would make him angry and she didn't want to do that, for he was one of the persistent kind. He wouldn't take no for an answer when he asked for a date. She realized that he had almost cut her off from every other boy, for they had taken it for granted that she was Harold's steady.

Winter came with blinding gusts of snow. The trees were laden and branches cracked under the heavy weight of ice and snow. The world seemed covered with a glistening robe of white.

Fortunately, as Christmas approached, the weather turned warmer and the gay Christmas parties became the order of the season. Beth faced a struggle with her conscience when she was invited to the big party and dance at the Holmes residence. The Holmes family was perhaps the wealthiest family in town and their parties were events that were always looked forward to with excitement by the ones fortunate enough to be invited.

When Beth mentioned the subject of her dress for the occasion, her mother looked grave.

"Beth, you know what kind of parties the Holmes' usually give. There is always dancing and drinking. I don't want you to go."

"But Mom!" Beth exclaimed. "I can't refuse to go. If I do, they will know the reason. At least Adelaide will and she's one of my best friends. I've never been invited before, for these parties have just been for the upper classmen and I've just become one. What can I tell her? That my mother thinks I'm too good to come to her party? That will make them angry with you and Mr. Holmes may fire Daddy from the plant."

"Mr. Holmes knows what your father believes and that he doesn't approve of drinking. He knows your father is a Christian and he respects him for what he stands for, even if he's not a Christian himself. That has nothing to do with you. If you go, you'll feel out of place, for you know there will be dancing. Can't you tell Adelaide that you don't dance?"

Beth looked guilty and her eyes fell before her mother's quiet gaze. Her mother recognized the symptoms, and knew that Beth was hiding something from her.

"You have been dancing, haven't you, while I thought that you never had learned how."

Beth nodded silently.

"How long have you known how to dance?" her mother asked quietly.

"Ever since I was a senior in high school," Beth admitted. "Oh, Mommy, can't you understand? I just couldn't sit around when all the others were dancing. I'd have been miserable. Laurie taught me how to dance. Why is it so wrong for me to dance? I don't belong to the church and I'm not a Christian, so why is it wrong?"

"You know without asking that, why I think it's wrong," her mother said.

Beth heard the hurt tone in her voice and it grieved her.

"Belonging to the church doesn't mean that something is right or wrong. It's God who sets the standards of right and wrong, not the church. You know that. And even if you're not a Christian, if you do wrong, you will be held accountable to God, unless you repent and ask for forgiveness. I've told you what grief and humiliation the dance has brought to so many, so it's no use repeating it. I won't refuse to let you go, for you're old enough to go your own way if you persist, but you know how it will grieve me for you to do the things that I think you shouldn't."

"Then I may go?" Beth asked hesitantly.

She hated to hurt her mother, but she just couldn't refuse that invitation. It meant too much to her.

"If you persist," her mother replied.

"How about my dress?" Beth asked, still more hesitantly.

"I'll see that you won't be ashamed of the way you look. I'll have your dress ready for you."

Beth put her arms around her mother and noticed tears in her eyes.

"Mommy, I don't want to hurt you, but can't you understand?" she pleaded.

"I shall try," her mother replied as she gently withdrew from Beth's arms.

Mrs. Harris went to her room and spent a while in tearful prayer that she might do the right thing where Beth was concerned and that she might have the wisdom to guide her without trying to force her to do what she should do. She knew that little could be gained by that method.

Beth was almost sorry that she had been invited to the party, though she knew that she would have been hurt if she hadn't been. She didn't want to hurt her mother, yet she knew that she had hurt her doubly by having deceived her about knowing how to dance.

The night of the party she looked lovely as usual in her dress of pale green with little rosebuds at the neck and trimming the puffed sleeves. She thanked her mother for the lovely dress and told her how much she loved her.

"I promise to be a good girl," she said, "and never to give you any cause for heartache, even if I'm not a Christian like you want me to be. I promise that I will be some day."

Her mother smiled and told her that she hoped she would have a good time, but that she wouldn't be too late getting home.

"I promise," Beth said. Then at the sound of the doorbell, she went to meet Harold.

Though she told herself that she was enjoying the evening, there was a constant gnawing of conscience as she remembered her mother's eyes that were troubled, in spite of her smile. Conscience smote her even more strongly as she remembered how gently, though sorrowfully, her mother had questioned her and had learned how she had deceived her about knowing how to dance. That was the way her mother had always been with her and she was grateful for it, gentle, though firm when she was younger and had to be controlled.

She had heard other girls tell how their mothers had bossed them and had been harsh with them. They told how, even now, they had used every art of deceit to keep their mothers from scolding them or forbidding them to do the things they wanted to do, but which their mothers knew they shouldn't do.

Remembering this made Beth feel even more uncomfortable as she knew how her mother had felt about this party. Yet she had not refused to make the dress for her, though she could have. She noticed, with a little feeling of pride, that her dress was as pretty as any of the others.

Mrs. Holmes had commented upon her appearance when she came in, and had told her how lovely she looked. Later she had remarked about Beth's dress.

"I'm sure your mother couldn't have made that lovely dress," she said. "Adelaide says she makes most of your clothes."

Her tone was rather patronizing and Beth resented it.

"Indeed she did make it," Beth told her. "I'd rather wear a dress that Mother makes, than to have one from the most expensive shop in town."

"I'm surprised that your mother let you come," Mrs. Holmes said. "She's such a straight-laced little person and such a strict church member, that I'm sure she doesn't approve of such parties as ours."

"My mother says I'm old enough to know what is right and what is wrong. She no longer treats me as if I were a little child. She knows that I'll never do anything that would bring shame or disgrace to her."

"You have a wonderful mother," Mrs. Holmes replied as Harold came to claim her for the dance.

Beth knew that she hadn't told Mrs. Holmes the whole truth. Though she might never do anything that would bring disgrace to her mother, she was doing something that had caused her much heartache and she felt uncomfortable as Harold held her too closely. She was suddenly aware of Harold's attitude in paying her so much attention. His eyes surveyed the room as they danced.

"Those girls are all jealous of you," he remarked as he continued to hold her too near. "You're the most beautiful girl in the room, and you've honored me by dancing with me so often."

"You think they're jealous of me because you show me so much attention," she replied, pulling away from him a little. "You're having a wonderful time because you make all the other boys angry by monopolizing me. The great hero condescends to show a little unknown his gracious favor."

"What on earth brought on that remark?" he asked in surprise. "I'm dancing with the queen because I ap-

41

preciate the honor you've bestowed on me by being my steady."

"I'm not your steady," she denied tartly, "so don't let that idea get around. I don't want all of my other friends to turn their back on me after all those years when they've been so nice to me."

"What's got into you tonight?" he asked. "Being queen must've gone to your head."

"No more than being hero of the ball field has gone to yours," she retorted.

"Thanks for that kind remark," he said angrily.

Just then someone came up to break in. Ordinarily Harold would have ignored him as he had done on other occasions, but now as Beth pulled away from him, he let her go and stalked across the room to break in on another couple.

"What's happened to your boy friend?" her partner asked. "He looked as if he'd had a knockout blow."

"I informed him that he wasn't my steady; that I didn't want all of my friends getting any wrong ideas about us," she told him.

"That's not what he's been telling us," he told her. "But it's just as well you've set me straight. The fellows will be glad to know that the queen is still available for dates. You're lucky you didn't let him take possession of you any longer, for that fellow has a roving eye and his favors never last long. He's a wandering boy friend."

Beth laughed at the remark as they floated over the smooth floor until the end of the dance.

During the rest of the evening, Harold let her alone while he bestowed his attention upon other girls who were thrilled that he was dancing with them. They cast eyes at Beth, but she didn't lack for attention. She was glad, however, when the evening was over and they were on their way home.

Harold scarcely said a word, and when she tried to start a conversation he answered in monosyllables, pouting like a child. When they reached home, she turned to him and gave him a smile.

"Thank you for a pleasant evening," she said, then added sarcastically, "and thanks for being so entertaining on the way home."

"Good night," he answered sullenly.

As she went to her room she thought of Gary. She hadn't thought of him all evening, but now his face rose before her and her heart melted. How different he was from this conceited boy who thought that every girl considered it an honor to be noticed by him.

Though she had enjoyed her brief period when she had been Harold's only date, she was glad that it was over and she was free again. Perhaps now Gary would be her friend again as in the old days when there was no one else who came in between them; when they were sufficient for each other. She almost wished that they were back in those old days again, when there were no problems to face, no decisions to make; when she just had to obey her mother and leave all the problems of life in her hands.

CHAPTER 7

Also in this Christmas season the young people of the church were rehearsing for a Christmas pageant. Beth had never been interested in any of the activities of the church, but this year she had been asked to take part in the pageant and, since she knew that it would please her mother, she accepted the part.

She was given the part of the virgin mother and she was surprised when she learned that Gary was to play the part of Joseph. She was pleased when she learned that she would sing several numbers during the pageant. She knew that this would please her mother and she was glad of the opportunity to do what she had always longed to do, to sing before a large audience.

Harold was still pouting with her and some of Beth's friends teased her about his sudden indifference. He had always been on hand when there was a chance for him to be with Beth. Beth only laughed at their teasing, though she didn't answer any of their questions. She rather enjoyed their curiosity.

She felt a sense of relief, and was more sorry than ever that some of the girls who had gone with Harold were still cool to her. She was sure that they would be glad to know that he had dropped her as he had dropped them. Since this was only partly true, she didn't mind, for she didn't lack for attention.

During rehearsals, she was, of course, in constant contact with Gary. She was happy about this, for she had seen so little of him since that night under the trees and she still felt the loss of his constant companionship.

She had very little to do in the way of acting. She and Gary would, of course, be beside the little manger where the Christ Child lay, she seated at one side and he standing at the other while they looked down in rapt admiration at the child.

Beth's mother was delighted that she had been chosen for the part, for she hoped that in some way the consciousness of what the Lord's birth meant to the world would strike a responsive chord in her heart and that she would at last be willing to yield her heart to Him.

On the night of the presentation of the pageant, the auditorium of the educational building was packed. The first scene showed the shepherds watching over their flocks when the angel appeared to them, while one of them uttered the words that have been read and remembered by thousands through the centuries, "Fear not, for I bring you good tidings of great joy, for behold unto you is born this day in the city of David a Saviour, which is Christ the Lord — and ye shall find the Babe wrapped in swaddling clothes and lying in a manger."

From behind the scene where the angel stood, there appeared a number of other angels and then their voices rang out in the familiar words, "Glory to God in the highest and on earth peace, good will to men."

During a short intermission someone played a beautiful violin solo, then the curtain was raised upon the scene in the cave where small figures of cattle stood in one corner while in the forefront stood the manger with the sleeping infant. Gary looked more handsome than ever, with his strong face glowing with an inner light as he looked down upon the figure of the child. His long Oriental robe touched the tops of his sandals as he bent over with folded hands.

Beth was more lovely than ever as her golden hair fell in soft shimmering waves about her face as she bent over the crib.

It didn't matter to the producer of the pageant that Mary very likely had dark hair. He wanted a lovely scene and he most surely had what he had planned. Her face was in profile as she looked down with a smile at the sleeping infant.

Presently, to the strains of soft music behind the scene, she began to sing, "Sleep, little one, sleep."

Her voice was low and tender and the vibrant melody of the exquisite tones touched the hearts of the audience and brought tears to the eyes of many.

Beth's mother wiped the tears away unashamedly. She had always been proud and thankful for the gift that God had given her child, but tonight she was doubly grateful and aware of its power to touch the hearts as she saw others wipe away a tear that had come.

When Beth had finished the song, voices were heard outside the cave wondering if this could be the place the angel had told them about. They came in hesitantly and doubtful until they saw the child with Mary and Joseph by His side. One of the younger boys had brought a little lamb and as the others knelt beside the manger, he added his adoration of the One whom the angels had proclaimed to be the Son of God for whom they had been looking and waiting.

As they knelt, Mary began to sing again, at first softly, then letting her voice swell to full power as she continued the beautiful Magnificat, "My Soul Doth Magnify the Lord."

Though the producer knew full well that Mary had sung this as she and Elizabeth had met before her Son was born, he felt that it would be too impressive to be left out. And he wanted to give the audience another opportunity to hear that lovely voice again.

Beth's mother was sitting near so that she couldn't help but see Gary's gaze as he looked at Beth while she sang. She knew that he was still in love with Beth and she prayed again that Beth would fall in love with him.

"Wow! What a voice you have!" Bob exclaimed as he and Laurie went with Beth toward their dressing rooms. "You ought to be in opera."

"Thanks a lot," Beth said while her heart beat with joy at his praise.

Gary met them as they came out a little later.

"May I walk home with you?" he asked. "Will you let me?"

"Of course she will," Laurie informed him. "She's longing to hear how you liked her singing. Aren't you, Beth?" she asked, laughing.

She was glad that Beth no longer went with Harold. She knew that he wasn't the kind of boy Beth should be going with. She had an older brother, and he had hinted to Laurie some things about Harold that made Laurie feel uneasy for Beth. She loved Beth and she didn't want to see her hurt.

Gary smiled at Laurie's interruption while he waited for Beth's reply.

"You have my permission," Beth told him with a smile.

She had seen the look in his eyes while she was singing, and that look had warmed her heart in a way that nothing that Harold had ever done or said had been able to do.

"I'll wait for you at the door," he said and left them, for he knew that Beth would be held up by so many, telling her how they had enjoyed her singing.

"I'd give a lot to see a boy look at me like he looked at you while you were singing," Laurie said as she uttered a sigh. "Instead of him worshiping the Christ child, he was worshiping you."

"Oh, stop being so silly," Beth replied.

"You're the one who'll be silly if you turn that boy down," Laurie retorted. "He's worth dozens of fellows like Harold Brandon."

"I have no intention of turning him down," Beth told her. "But he may turn me down."

"Not a chance!" Laurie ejaculated.

As Beth and Gary walked the short distance to her home, Beth clinging to his arm, they said nothing for a while. Each was absorbed in his own thoughts. Finally Beth broke the silence.

"I'm happy that I took part in that pageant. I never thought I'd enjoy being in it as much as I did. I just took the part to please Mom."

"You were more beautful than I've ever seen you," he said slowly. "I thought that last song was the most beautiful song I'd ever heard."

"Thank you," she said, thrilled at his words.

He was not given to praise very often and he had never praised her so lavishly. It sent a warm glow through her and her heart was singing a little song. He loved her and she loved him. She had known all along that she did, but the love she now felt for him was different from what she had felt before. She had not realized that it was this love which had made her miss him so when he had tried to withdraw from her life. She had thought that it was just because he had been a part of it for so long. But now this was quite different, and the awareness of it left her startled, though quite happy.

"I wonder if you can imagine what I was thinking as I stood by that crib, listening to you sing, and watching you while you bent over and looked down at the baby?" Gary asked.

"I couldn't. What were you thinking?"

"I was thinking how wonderful it would be if that scene wasn't just a make-believe affair, but that it was really you and I looking down at our little one." His tones were low and vibrant. "If that were true, only heaven could make me happier."

"Why Gary!" she gasped, too astonished to say more.

He stopped and put his arm around her there in the darkness and drew her gently to him. She didn't resist, but remained in his arms while he held her close.

"You know how much I love you, how I've always

48

loved you. My little boy worship has grown with the years. Tonight I almost felt like an idolator as I stood there looking at you while you sang. I used to think you cared for me as much as I cared for you. Was there one little spark of love for me then? If there was, is there no little spark left in your heart for me?" he asked tenderly.

"There is, Gary, not just a little spark, but a great big flame. I love you! I love you! I never realized that I did until you began to stay away from me. But I know now that I do."

She raised her face for his kiss and their lips met and clung there while joy flowed through her.

"Your voice is the gift of God, my darling," he said when he had released her. "How wonderful it would be, if you would use it for the Lord. Singing His praises with a voice like yours could win thousands to Him."

"But I'm not even won myself," she objected.

"I pray God that you soon will be," he said fervently. "How wonderful if you could yield your life as well as your talent solely to Him."

"I wish for your sake that I could," she said in a faraway voice. "But I can't. Not just yet. I've got my youth and my life to live before I give up everything and let God take over. There's too much that I would have to give up if I did that."

"But He would give you much more than you would have to give up," he argued earnestly. "Believe me, you'd soon see how foolish you were not to have yielded your life to Him long ago."

"Please don't kill all the joy of tonight by talking like that," she begged. "I want to be foolish a little while longer. I don't want to use my voice for the Lord. I want to use it for myself for a little while. I want to sing before great audiences, greater than that little crowd there tonight. That's the ambition of my life. I don't want to hurt you, Gary, because I do love you very much. But that's the way I feel and I just don't want to feel any different. Give me time, Gary, give me time."

"How do you know you'll have time?" he persisted sorrowfully. "Our time as well as our life is in God's hands. Think about that, Beth. Nothing I can say will change you. I'll just have to leave you in God's hands and keep on praying for you."

He bent over and kissed her lightly and murmured a low good night.

"Oh, Gary! I'm sorry! I'm sorry!" she cried in distress.

He didn't answer, but stumbled away in the darkness like a man who was carrying an agonizing wound.

As she turned toward the door, there were tears in her eyes. The joy of her triumph of the evening and the greater joy she had experienced when she was held in his arms and felt his lips upon hers, were all gone. Only sorrow remained and a hurt that was greater than physical pain. There was no desire to change her mind and to repent and ask God's forgiveness and salvation, just the stubborn determination to fulfill her ambition in life.

CHAPTER 8

Beth's mother met her at the door. Her eyes were shining.

"I was so proud of you, dear," she said as she put her arms around Beth. "You sang more beautifully than you ever sang before. There were many people who had tears in their eyes and I know I had tears in mine. I'm so glad that you took that part, for no one else could have done it as well. The Lord has given you a great talent, darling, a great gift, and I do pray that some day soon you will use it for Him."

"I'm glad you liked me in the part, Mom," Beth said.

Her mother's words smote her with keen pain, for they seemed an echo of what Gary had said. She knew that, much as Gary loved her, he would never want to marry her until she yielded her life to the Lord. She also knew that, much as she loved him, she would never give up her determination to satisfy her ambition. She had always hoped to become a concert singer, though that attainment seemed very far off. Still she was determined to live her life with that aim in view. She knew, from her mother's teaching, that she couldn't serve God and her worldly ambition at the same time, and just now, all she wanted was worldly ambition.

She had been asked several times to join the choir in her church, and had refused, but after what had happened following the pageant, she decided that it would please her mother and perhaps please Gary if she should join. So Beth joined the choir. Her mother was delighted, and the still small voice of conscience was silenced for the time being.

Laurie and the others were delighted when she came to choir practice and asked if she might sing with them. The choir director was overjoyed, for he needed a good soprano, and he knew that he couldn't find a better one than Beth.

It was on Easter morning that Beth sang her first solo. It was a difficult one, for it ran into the high notes of the register. She sang it with such ease that the notes seemed to flow from her lips without any effort. She took the high notes with sweetness as well as depth.

Her mother listened with a grateful heart, for she felt that at last Beth was beginning to turn her life in the right direction. How little she knew of the truth of what was in Beth's heart and mind.

Just before the communion, Beth sang a hymn. When she had been chosen to sing at this time, she had asked that she might choose the song. When the clear young voice rang out in soft, pure tones that held a depth of reverence, the congregation listened with rapt attention.

"I'd rather have Jesus than anything," she sang, until the last warm note drifted into the hearts of those listening. Beth's mother covered her face for a moment, for she couldn't keep back the tears. If Beth only meant in her heart what she sang with such reverence! How could she sing like that and not really mean in her heart what her voice was singing so beautifully! Perhaps she was beginning to turn her thoughts to the Lord. How she prayed that this was true!

As Beth looked over the congregation while she sang, she saw Gary, and in his eyes, she saw, even at that distance, that same light that she had noticed the night of the pageant.

Sitting nearby, she noticed a stranger who was with Laurie and her parents. It was not until the next day that she learned who the stranger was. She had forgotten all about him in the meantime. Laurie phoned Beth early the next morning.

"I've got something to tell you that'll knock you over, so you'd better sit down," Laurie's excited voice said.

"Don't keep me waiting. Let me have it," Beth urged.

"Did you see that man who was sitting with us in church yesterday morning?" Laurie asked.

"I believe I did," Beth replied, not quite sure that she did remember. "What's he got to do with all your exciting news?"

"Plenty. He's connected with some recording firm and he wants to meet you and get a recording of your voice. Just think, if he thinks it's good enough, you might have a record made. And it might become a best seller," Laurie enthused.

"Whew! Do you think he really means it?" Beth asked as her excitement mounted.

"Sure he means it. Can you come over this evening? He's going to be at our house. He and Dad were chums at college. He was passing through and stopped off just to see us, and also went to church with us. He thinks he's made a discovery in you, honey."

"Wow!" Beth exclaimed. "Wouldn't that be something! I'll be over this evening, sure."

"Guess what, Mom!" she cried as soon as she had hung up. "I'm going to have a test of my voice made for a record."

Her mother stared at her in speechless surprise while Beth told her what Laurie had said.

"You don't look a bit happy," Beth said, disappointed. "Just think what that may mean, Mom. My big chance! It's what I've been hoping and dreaming all my life."

"I don't know whether I should be happy," her mother said truthfully. "I'm so astonished that I can't think."

"Mom! How can you act like that?" Beth cried, disappointed and hurt. "I should think that you'd be glad that someone likes my voice well enough to want to make a recording of it."

"I am glad that someone likes your voice that well," her mother told her. "But you know how I feel about your ambition. Why repeat it?"

"No. Please don't," Beth sighed. "This may be my one big chance and I want that more than anything else in the world."

"Yes, I know," her mother agreed sadly. "I just hope and pray that you won't regret making that one thing your whole aim in life."

Beth didn't answer, but left the room, while her mother looked after her sorrowfully.

"She's in Your hands, Lord," she whispered. "Only You can make her change her mind. No matter what it takes, I pray that You will lead her to the place where she will be willing to turn her life over to You."

In the light of what would follow through the years, she might have wondered if she would still be willing to repeat those words.

After Beth had helped her mother with the dishes, she dressed and hurried over to Laurie's. She had been unusually quiet during the meal. Her parents had followed their usual conversation but presently her father turned to her.

"Why so silent, honey?" he asked. "You've scarcely said a word."

"She's thinking about where she's going tonight," her mother answered for her. "She's to meet a man at Laurie's who's going to give her a test for a recording."

"That's wonderful!" he exclaimed. "Why didn't you tell me about it?"

"I thought Mom would rather tell you," she replied.

"Beth thinks it's her great chance," her mother told him. "I'm happy for her and I hope that she gets good results with the test."

Beth looked at her mother in surprise, but said nothing.

After Beth had left, her father turned to his wife.

"What's the mystery about all this?" he asked. "There's something wrong. What is it?"

"Beth was disappointed because I wasn't enthusiastic about this. I'm wondering if it is best for her."

"Aren't you just a bit too pessimistic over Beth's ambition?'

"Perhaps I am," she admitted. "Let's hope and pray for the best for her and for her soul."

Beth was so excited that she almost ran over to Laurie's, and was out of breath when she arrived. Both of Laurie's parents were there when she met Mr. Candler. They were almost as excited as the girls were.

"I'll come to the point at once," Mr. Candler said when they were seated. "I heard you sing yesterday and I think you have great possibilities. My firm makes recordings for prospective young actresses and singers. Talent scouts are constantly on the lookout for those who have talent as well as the beauty you have." He gave her a smile.

"Thank you," Beth said breathlessly, overwhelmed by his words.

"I'm sorry I have to hurry you. I wish I had more time, but my plane leaves shortly and I want to be sure that the arrangements I've made with a local firm here will be satisfactory to you. They will make a recording of your voice on tape. Laurie tells me that you also play the piano as well as a few other instruments."

"She can play anything," Laurie offered, interrupting.

"I do play the piano," Beth told him. "And whatever arrangements you make will certainly be all right with me."

"They will tape both your voice and then your piano music. You may take the time to prepare for the audition. Those tapes will be sent on to us and I'll pass them on to our experts. If they think it advisable, we'll arrange for you to have an audition in our recording department, then we'll have an interview with some motion picture or TV company. After that we'll see what comes of it. Let's hope that it will be something really good."

Beth was speechless. Her dream seemed to be coming true, but she wondered what her parents would say about her going away for that other recording. She was afraid that they would object.

"Suppose you sing something for me," Mr. Candler suggested.

Beth went to the piano. Her fingers ran idly over the keys while she tried to think of what she could sing. Mr. Candler knew at once that she had talent for playing the piano which was far above the average.

She began to sing a simple little ballad. When she finished that, while she regained her composure in the face of this overwhelming realization of her dreams, she sang a more difficult number which took her voice through the higher register.

When she had finished, there was silence for a moment. Then Mr. Candler remarked, "You have what it takes, young lady. I predict a great future for you."

She gave him a radiant smile. "I hope your prediction comes true."

They talked for a while longer, then Mr. Candler rose to leave.

"I shall be eagerly awaiting that tape and the report when it's played before our committee," he told Beth.

He gave her further instructions and the address of the recording company, then he bade them all good-by and left.

When he was gone, Laurie turned to Beth. "Isn't that wonderful!" she cried. "Just think, if you hadn't joined the choir, this never would have happened."

"I can't believe that it really has happened," Beth replied, still dazed at the prospect that this interview held.

On her way home, she was still trying to comprehend and to realize that it was really true and not just a dream. It was the beginning of a dream come true — the dream of a lifetime.

CHAPTER 9

Beth decided not to tell her mother about the possible trip to New York. She would wait and let that problem take care of itself, if it should arise. She surely hoped that she would be called upon to go. She did tell her, however, how enthusiastic Mr. Candler was about both her singing and piano playing. Her mother tried to appear pleased and not to put a damper upon Beth's high spirits, no matter how she herself might feel about the whole affair. Perhaps she was, as her husband had suggested, feeling to pessimistic about it. She would leave it all to the Lord.

The recording company did their utmost to produce a good tape for Beth and they too were quite lavish in their praise and hopes for the future. After she has finished there, she went to the photographer that Mr. Candler had made arrangements with and had several photos taken.

In the background of her thoughts, during all of these arrangements, was the thought of her mother. She wouldn't let this thought dampen her spirits, but still that little voice of conscience made her uneasy. Even though her mother might not prevent her from doing the thing she dearly wanted to do, she knew that her mother only felt as she did because she wanted Beth to have the best in life, even though that best might not be the thing that Beth wanted to do. She silenced that voice once more in her stubborn determination to do everything in her power and to take advantage of every opportunity that would lead her to her goal as a concert singer. If it was by way of TV or pictures, she would take it.

When her father asked her about the result of her visit to the studio, she told him that they liked her voice and that they gave her much encouragement about the record. He seemed greatly pleased and told her so. Her mother listened quietly and when he asked her what she thought about it, she said that she was glad that they liked Beth's voice and she hoped that the recording would be a success. She did not say what was in her heart — that this might just be another step that Beth would take which might lead her away from God. She would try to be patient and not despair, no matter what might happen, for she believed in God, and in her prayer, that somehow, someday, He would lead Beth in the path she should follow.

Laurie lost no time in spreading the news about Beth's big chance and Beth was swamped with congratulations and questions. Harold Brandon was among the boys who wished her well.

Beth was surprised to see him, for she had not had a talk with him since the night of the dance and she thought that she was out of his life permanently. He waited until the others had left before he spoke to her.

"The queen must be holding court again," he remarked. "I thought I'd have to ask for an appointment for an audience."

"I didn't think you would care for an audience," she told him.

"I came to ask forgiveness for the way I acted that night," he said with an unfamiliar note of humility.

"Your apology is accepted, my lord," she retorted mischievously.

"Then let me offer my congratulations. I hear that there are great things in store for you."

"I think that Laurie has counted chickens before they're hatched," she said seriously. "I'm sorry she spread such a glowing report about me. I'm not building any air castles that might come tumbling down and leave me disappointed."

"I'm not afraid about your succeeding," he said. "I was at church, believe it or not, and when I heard you sing, I knew that you had a great future if you wanted it, for your voice is out of this world."

"Thank you for saying such a nice thing," and she gave him a smile. "I love to sing and I'd rather be a success as a singer than anything else."

"How about going to the game with me Saturday? There's a Little League game between our town high school team and Crossman's over in Edgewood."

"I'll have to let you know," she told him. "May I let you know tomorrow?"

"Of course," he replied, looking somewhat disappointed. Girls usually jumped at the chance for a date with him.

"I want to ask Mother if it'll be all right for me to go," she informed him.

"Great guns! You don't still have to ask your mother if you can go places, do you? I thought you had outgrown that."

"I always help her with the housework on Saturdays," she explained. "We don't have any outside help. And I do consult with my mother about my dates. I don't ever expect to outgrow that."

He didn't answer, and they separated as they entered the building for their classes.

Beth had hoped to see Gary. She wondered how he would accept the news of her probable success with the recording company. She was sure that he felt the same way her mother did, but she wanted to talk to him anyway. She wanted to tell him that, even if this led to success, she loved him and that if he would wait for her for just a little while, until she had her brief taste of success, she would be willing to do what he had said was the one thing that had kept them apart.

She met him late that afternoon as they came from

the auditorium, where there had been a student assembly.

"I've missed you," she told him as they left the campus. "You've disappeared from my life again, this time completely."

"Isn't that the way it should be?" he asked gravely.

"No, it isn't," she insisted. "Can't we keep on being friends, even if you've made up your mind not to care anymore?"

"You know I haven't done that," he replied. "But I didn't want to intrude. I wanted to leave the field open so that you could have all the admirers and the happy times that you insist you must have. You might not have them if I kept hanging around. You could forget me."

"But I don't want to forget you," she insisted. "You don't believe that I love you, but I do. I want you, no matter how many others I have who want to date me. You're leaving me out of your life."

"You're leaving me out," he contradicted. "You say you love me, but you don't really, not in the way I love you. If you did, you would be willing to do the one thing that would make it possible for us to be together in our love. You love your ambition more than you love me or anyone else, so why need we talk about love anymore?"

"I suppose you know what Laurie had been telling everyone," she offered.

"Yes, I heard, and that only confirms what I've already said. You care more for your singing and your possible career than you ever will care for me or for the Lord."

"That's not true," she stated emphatically, clinging to him as they walked along. "I love you ever so much. But why can't I have both? If you love me so much why can't you wait just a little while, until I've had my little fling at fame? You'll be at graduate school and we wouldn't be together. In the meantime, I could have a little fun if I'm a success as a singer. Then we could

60

be together. I know you've never asked me to marry you," she said with a little embarrassed laugh, "but I'd be willing to wait for you, if you'd only ask me to wait."

Her voice was vibrant with its appeal and it stirred him to the depths. He longed to take her in his arms and tell her that he would wait for years, if it would bring them together, but he knew that he dared not. If he did that just now, all of his will power would melt with the touch of her lips, and he knew that what she proposed was not the thing that God would have him do.

"You're asking something that would never be possible, Beth," he said, trying to keep his voice steady and not reveal the great strain he was under. "You talk as if, following your fling and your willingness to settle down for the Lord, God would be there just waiting for you and would be willing to take what was left of your life. How little you're making God! Jesus said 'I stand at the door and knock,' but God said that His spirit would not always strive with man. Jesus is knocking, but if you turn Him away, one day you may never again hear that knock. If you wait until you are ready, it may be too late, Beth, my darling. God's Word says that His time is now. 'Now is the day of salvation.'"

She was silent while she fought back the tears. She wanted him now, in this moment, more than she wanted fame or ambition.

"Don't you see that I wouldn't hold you to any promise," he continued, "as long as you turn away from God's pleading? It wouldn't be fair to you or to me. While I'd be aching with longing for you, you might find someone else who would attract you in your new life. I wouldn't hold you to a promise that you might want to break. It would only bring heartache to both of us. I can only try to be happy in my work and pray that someday, before it's too late, you may answer that knocking at your heart's door and say that you're willing to be my wife on the only terms that I can offer you."

They had reached her home and she was fighting back the tears.

"Good-by, Gary," she murmured brokenly as she turned away to keep him from seeing her tears.

He saw the tears and there were tears in his heart as he said, "Good-by, my darling, and may the Lord be merciful and bless you."

As he walked away, he fought the desire to turn back and take her in his arms and tell her that he'd marry her, no matter how long he had to wait, no matter whether she turned to the Lord or not. But he kept doggedly on, knowing that he was walking in the strength of the Lord and not in his own strength.

Beth closed the door quietly and crept to her room where she gave way to tears and the sobs that she had struggled to keep from bursting forth. Just now ambition seemed a drab, useless thing, but she knew that it would return again, a glittering bauble which would lead her on, perhaps to joy, perhaps to heartache. Now there was only heartache.

CHAPTER 10

Beth waited impatiently to hear from Mr. Candler, but as the days passed into weeks and she heard nothing, her spirits drooped and she finally gave up hope. His associates must not have cared for the tape.

She felt embarrassed when her friends asked her from time to time if she had heard any news. She tried to explain that these things took time, but they didn't believe her explanation. Laurie, who was more interested in the outcome, was worried and disappointed, but she tried to keep Beth encouraged.

Beth had gone with Harold to a game or two before the term examinations began, but neither of them seemed interested in keeping up the friendship which had started with such a sudden spurt. Harold went with other girls at the same time that he was going occasionally with her, but Beth didn't mind, and she took the good-natured teasing from her friends because she didn't care what Harold did. She had lost interest in him.

She was hurt because Gary avoided her. They met occasionally on their way to classes, but there was never time for conversation. Gary was pleasantly friendly, the same kind, gentle friend, but he never gave her any encouragement that they could be more than friends. He was doing what he said he felt he should do — eliminate himself from her life.

This attitude, together with the disappointment about the tests, made her morose and unhappy. Her father noticed it and remarked about it.

"What's happened between you and Gary?" he asked. "He hasn't been around for so long. Have you two had a quarrel?"

"No. He's just busy with his studies. He's taking extra work so that when he enters graduate school, he'll cut his time short."

"He used to come often and frequently stayed for dinner, but now he never does. I miss him."

"So do I," Beth admitted, while she smiled feebly. "I invited him once or twice, but he had to go home and study. He surely had a pile of books in his arms."

When the final examinations began, Beth was too much absorbed in her own studies to think about Gary or the tapes. She had always excelled in her grades, and she didn't want to fall behind. She was pleased when she received her report from the examinations, to know that she passed with flying colors.

She was now a senior. In one more year she would be out of college and on her own, and she was determined to get a position somewhere where she could use her musical talent. She knew that she would have to work, for she didn't want to continue to be dependent upon her parents. Still she wanted to do the thing she loved most. She felt that she would never hear from Mr. Candler. That dream was ended.

She was asked to sing a solo at the commencement exercises. She was not too enthusiastic, but she agreed to sing.

Her song was the highlight of the program. She was lovely, as usual, in her simple white dress while the seniors sat nearby in their black robes.

She saw Gary not far away. This was his great day, for he was now a graduate and on his way to the beginning of a teaching career. She knew, as she caught a brief glimpse of him while she sang, that he still loved her, even if he had tried to take his presence out of her life. He couldn't hide what he felt for her in that moment when he was not aware that she saw him.

He would soon be leaving for graduate school, and

she looked forward to a dull summer, with hopes blasted and dreams ended.

Gary was the valedictorian and he delivered his message with quiet assurance and without any evidence of nervousness. He finished to the thunderous applause of the audience.

They met as they were leaving the auditorium.

"Let me congratulate you on your valedictory message," she said. "You were wonderful, and I was so proud to know that you were my friend. I thought of the years past when we had been together and I just couldn't realize that it was my own little playmate who had become a man of such great capabilities. Again, let me offer my congratulations."

"You overwhelm me," he said, smiling down at her.

"I suppose you'll be leaving soon for summer school," she remarked as others came toward them to offer their congratulations.

"In a couple of weeks," he told her. Then they were interrupted by friends flocking around him and she left him, feeling that she had lost something even more precious than the dream she had also lost.

A day or so later, when she was feeling blue and forsaken, a letter came from New York. She opened it with fingers that trembled while her heart skipped a beat as she read the contents. It was from Mr. Candler, and he explained why it had taken him so long to let her know the result of the tapes.

He said that he had been called to the west coast to make arrangements for some tests out there, and that he had been ill after that and unable to continue his work with the firm.

"I have good news for you. Your tape was well-received by one of our recording companies. The motion picture business is at somewhat of a standstill just now, and they are not looking for new talent such as you have. If you can come to New York sometime in the near future, I think I can arrange for a test to be made for you to make a record. Your voice sounded wonderful and your photo was lovely. I was pleased to see that you are quite photogenic. So many lovely girls are not.

"If you prove to have any acting ability, I predict a possible future for you on TV. Perhaps later there might be an entry into motion pictures, if what they see on the screen impresses motion picture talent scouts."

When Beth finished reading the letter, she dashed down to tell her mother the wonderful news.

"Mom! Oh Mom!" she cried, forgetting for the moment that her good news might not be good news to her mother. "I've got wonderful news! Mr. Candler wants me to come to New York for further tests. If I go over, I may get a chance to get into TV. Isn't that wonderful?"

Her mother's heart sank, but she tried not to let Beth see how she felt.

"I'm glad for you, if that's what you want," she said, but her smile wasn't too reassuring and Beth knew that she wasn't happy.

"Will it be all right with you if I do go to New York for the tests?" she asked hesitantly.

"If your father is willing for you to have the money," she said. "It's up to him."

"I have enough saved for a bus trip," Beth told her as the joy suddenly faded. "I think I can manage to pay my way for a little while. Those tests ought not to take long."

"I hate to see you go there alone," her mother said, "but see what your father says and then do what you think you should do."

"Mom, I know how you feel about this," Beth said penitently, "but can't you see? It's what I've longed for and dreamed about ever since I was old enough to have dreams. This is my one big chance. Just let me take it. It may not amount to anything, but do let me take that chance. I promise that if I'm a success, I'll just take a little fling at what I've longed for, then I'll settle down to be what you want me to be."

Her mother gave her a smile and kissed her.

"Wait and see what your father says. Now go and let me get dinner ready."

She knew that it was useless to say more, but her heart was heavy. She knew how her mother felt and the little voice of conscience was again whispering to her.

When her father came home and was told the news, he uttered an exclamation.

"Why, you've got me flabbergasted! I can't believe that my little girl might be on her way to fame and fortune."

"Then you'll say that I can go?" Beth asked eagerly as her spirits rose.

"That's up to your mother," he told her. "Whatever she says goes with me."

"But Mom has put it up to you," Beth argued. "If you say it's all right, she'll not object to my going."

He looked at his wife. He could see the sorrow in her eyes and it hurt him. They had talked it over again when the tapes were made and he knew just how she felt. He was willing to let Beth have "her fling," believing that in the end she would come back to her mother's way of thinking and would yield her life to the Lord. He knew that his wife did not share his confidence.

"What about it, honey?" he asked her.

"I won't make any objections if you don't," she told him.

He turned to Beth and said gravely, "You know how your mother feels, child, so if you want to do something that will hurt her, I won't try to stop you. Think it over before you make your decision."

"I've already thought it over and I want to go, Dad," Beth said stubbornly. "It may be my one great chance to do something with my voice and I'm not willing to let it pass. I don't want to hurt you and Mother, but I must go. I'll never be happy if I have to turn it down."

"I hope you'll never regret what you're so determined to do," he said heavily. "I won't try to stop you, but I hope that you will fail to go over in this test, whatever it is. I feel that in the end, you'll be glad that you failed."

"At least I want to try," she persisted.

The meal that evening was a rather silent, unhappy occasion.

CHAPTER 11

Beth's conscience kept whispering to her that she shouldn't hurt her mother by her determination to go to New York, but she refused to listen to that whisper. She couldn't miss this opportunity to make her dream come true. Another one like this might never come again.

Her mother tried to appear cheerful, and she never said another word to Beth about her fears for her.

Beth had sufficient clothes, and tears came to her eyes as she surveyed her wardrobe and remembered the hours her mother had put in while making them. When she packed her suitcase for the short trip, she included one of her prettiest formals, for she didn't know what might be required of her.

Laurie was thrilled when Beth told her that she was really going to New York. She was delighted that she had been the means of giving this opportunity to Beth and she was busy again on the telephone, spreading the news among their friends.

Beth's father was grave and silent, something unusual for him, for he was usually so gay and talkative. To Beth the house seemed more like the aftermath of a funeral than a time of rejoicing over her success thus far.

She refused to understand why her mother felt as she did about this great opportunity. She thought it was foolish of her mother to fear the danger that might come to her. She was sure that she was able to cope with any situation that might arise as a temptation in a possible professional life. She wasn't thinking of the spiritual side of life. She was thinking only of the moral side.

She thought that she wouldn't be able to see Gary before she left, for he had gone to make his arrangements for entrance into summer school. To her joy he returned the day before her departure. Laurie phoned her that she had seen Gary coming from the station. She knew that Beth would want to see him before she left. Beth phoned him at once and asked him if he wouldn't come over for a little while that evening. It would be their last time together.

He came and they sat out in the swing in the early darkness.

"I was hoping I would see you before I went away," she told him. "It will be so long before you return from summer school."

"I'm glad that I made it back so that I could see you before you embark on your great adventure."

"I'm so excited that I haven't been able to sleep," she said. "My dreams seem about to come true at last."

She didn't notice his serious face in the darkness.

"And if they don't, what then?" he asked.

"I'll still keep on hoping and dreaming, until they do."

"And after that?" he persisted in that same serious voice.

"If I succeed, I'll hope to become famous. I'll be what I've always dreamed of becoming, a concert singer, entertaining large audiences."

"And then what?" the quiet voice still questioned.

"Why, then I'll have a lot of money and I'll be able to give Mom and Dad the things that they've never been able to have."

"I wonder if they would accept money you've earned in that way," he remarked. Then in a voice infinitely sad, "Is that all that life means to you, Beth? Having fame and money? When you've reached the top and have those things, then what?"

"Then what?" she repeated sharply. "What do you mean by that?" She was hurt and angry by his questions and that last remark.

"I mean just that. Then what? When you have reached the top, there will be no place to go but down the other side of the slope. And your life will be empty and there will no longer be any joy of achievement."

"You surely do paint a dismal picture," she replied coldly.

"Isn't that the picture of all who have given their lives and their very souls to reach the top, with never a thought but their ambition? Look at the story of many in the professional world of music and acting. In a few short years after they have reached the top, they begin to slip and before long they are forgotten, with nothing to sustain them but blasted hopes and dreams long since past. They're out and done for. Many of them have spent all their living and end up in homes for the penniless or else in suicide. Is that the goal for which you're striving?"

"Yes it is," she retorted angrily. "When I've had success, I'll be satisfied to take the slump. I'll have my dreams of the days when I was on top and a success."

"Then what will you have to look forward to? Growing old and bitter, just dreaming of a success that is long gone and no longer brings you joy? Is that what you look forward to?"

"Oh, you're impossible!" she cried angrily. "I'm sorry you came, if that's all the encouragement you can give me."

He drew her to him in spite of her resistance, for, even though he had made her angry, she wanted to be held in his arms, to feel his kiss upon her lips for perhaps a long last time. The thought of being separated from him during the long summer months was the only thing that marred her perfect joy.

"I'm only trying to make you see that you're chasing a rainbow and that, even if you should find the end of it, there is no pot of gold there, but only sorrow and bitterness when success has vanished and you're left on the sidelines, forgotten and forsaken by a fickle public. There is a way of life that is so much better

71

than what you're trying to follow. If you would only use your talent and beauty in service to the God who gave them to you, the way would grow brighter and you would still be climbing to the top of the slope, for it never turns downward."

"A life like that never could bring me joy," she remarked, though she was stirred by his words.

"You never have given it a chance. You might never win fame, but you would be winning many precious souls who would rejoice through all eternity that you had lived. They would be the jewels that you would offer your Saviour when you kissed His feet and heard Him say 'Well done, good and faithful servant.' You could win thousands to Him with your voice and those songs that you sing with so much feeling."

"And where would I find those thousands?" she asked, sarcastically. She was no longer angry, but uneasy and suddenly very unhappy.

"Wherever God might lead you. There are so many revival services where you could be such a help to the evangelist. There would be those great open-air meetings where you could sing to larger audiences that you'd ever have in Carnegie Hall or some other entertainment place. And you'd never grow old and forgotten, for with your age would come a deeper experience and a greater power.

"I'm thinking of a tenor who still has a wonderful voice, though he is well over seventy. He's been singing for the Lord since he was a youth. He had many offers to go into operatic work, but he chose to give back to God what God had given to him. What a glory it will be when he meets his Lord! He's not sitting back and thinking of successes long since vanished. He's looking forward and up to the slope whose top reaches heaven. Your life could be like that, Beth, if you'd only surrender it to the Lord and give Him a chance with your life."

While she listened to his long speech, in her heart there was a struggle when ambition and yielding to God fought a desperate battle. Ambition finally won and she withdrew from his arms without having received his kiss. She shook her head slowly.

"I can't see it that way," she said. "You make it sound wonderful, but I'm committed to meeting Mr. Candler, and I'll go and see what he has to offer. Perhaps I'll fail, and if I do, I'll think about what you've said. Perhaps then, I'll do what you say I should do."

"I'm afraid you won't fail," he said, and his voice revealed something of the pain in his heart. "You've made your decision. God won't take second place in your life, unless He chastens you first. You can't turn your back upon Him and expect Him to receive you with open arms when you've failed in your goal in life that has left Him out of the picture. I pray that you won't regret the decision you've made. It's the last appeal I can make. I pray that the Lord will have mercy and bring you to Him, no matter what the cost to you, for your soul is at stake and it's more important than fame or wealth. I hope that you will not live to regret that you have missed the best when it may be too late. Then you'll realize that what I've said is true."

He rose to leave, but she held him back. She put her arms around his neck and again he folded her in his embrace.

"Kiss me good-by, Gary," she begged, and she held up her lips for his kiss. "Please wish me success."

He put his cheek against hers but he didn't kiss her. He knew that if he did, he would be crying like a baby and he didn't want to do that.

"I shall pray that you will have all that God intends for you and that you will yield your life to Him before it is too late," he said tenderly. "Good-by, my darling."

He released her and went quickly down the steps. She stood looking after him until he disappeared in the darkness while the tears streamed down her face. As she stood there, she was fighting the battle once more. Ambition won again. Slowly she turned and went into the house.

Her mother saw the tears as Beth passed on the way to her room and she once more uttered a prayer for Beth. She went to her room and wept upon her knees as she prayed that Beth would choose the right path before it was too late. Only time and her faith in God would tell.

CHAPTER 12

Beth's mother went with her to the station where she was to take the bus. Her father had insisted that she should let him give her the money to go by train, but she had refused to take the money. She felt guilty enough and she couldn't let him make the sacrifice that would be necessary if she took the money.

As he kissed her before he left for work, he held her for a few moments while tears blinded his eyes. His voice was husky as he said soberly, "I'll be praying for your safe journey and that God will take care of you. I just hope that you'll never be sorry you did what you're doing."

When he released her, he hurried away, so that she wouldn't see the tears he tried to conceal.

As she and her mother left for the station, Beth hoped that she could see Gary for one last moment at least. Her longing for him tugged at her heart and she almost wished that she wasn't leaving. She felt as if she were leaving home for the last time and it gave her a sickening sensation.

She had only a little while before time to get on the bus when they arrived. Her mother held her for a moment, then kissed her good-by.

"I'll be praying for you, honey," she murmured. "May God give you journeying mercies and may you have all that is best for you."

She also turned away so that Beth couldn't see the tears that began to flow.

Just as she was standing in line behind the others to

board the bus, Gary joined her. He had been standing nearby, watching her with hungry eyes. He felt as if he were seeing her for the last time and in his heart there were tears, though he managed a smile as he approached.

"I was wishing you'd come," she admitted as he joined her.

"I couldn't let you go without telling you good-by and wishing you every happiness. I shall miss you terribly."

"But I'll only be gone for a few days," she said. "You talk as if I'll never come back."

"Who knows what may happen? You may be an overnight sensation and be too busy to even give the old town a brief look. Then I may be very busy getting ready to leave for summer school and I may not be here when you return."

"I hope you will be here when I come back. I shall miss you all the long summer. Life will be so dull without you."

She saw the look in his eyes that always stirred her heart to quicker beating, but he didn't answer.

The line moved forward and as she approached the steps, he gave her a warm clasp and whispered, "May God bless and keep you." Then he was gone and she entered the bus and took the only available seat. It was on the far side so she couldn't even wave to him.

It was a long and tedious trip, and when she finally reached New York she was tired and worn. She felt bewildered as she got off and followed the crowd to wait for her luggage. Mr. Candler was supposed to meet her, but when she entered the waiting room, she didn't see him and panic seized her. What if he didn't come? What should she do? She didn't know how she could reach him, if he didn't appear. She sat down and waited nervously and impatiently for him to come. The crowd surged around her, making her more nervous and confused. She wished that she was back home and wondered if, after all, she had done right in coming here.

Finally, after nearly an hour of nervous waiting, Mr. Candler appeared. He hastened to her with apologies for being late.

"I was held up at the office and then the traffic delayed me," he explained.

"I was beginning to be afraid that you wouldn't come and I wondered what I should do," she admitted.

He had her bag taken to his car and they drove away to his office. He didn't tell her the big news until they were inside and she had had time to get adjusted. During the ride he had entertained her by pointing out various places of interest as they passed.

"I have a big surprise for you," he told her when they had been seated and she was calm again. "You just arrived in the nick of time. A day later and you would have missed what I believe will be a big start for you."

"What is it?" she asked excitedly.

She could tell by his manner and the smile that went with the words that something really wonderful was about to happen.

"To begin with," he said, "your voice was excellent and everyone was pleased just as I was when I first heard you sing for me. While I was waiting and hoping to hear from someone who might be interested in giving you a chance, one of the TV companies here on location ran into difficulty. One of their regular cast, a girl who had a lovely singing voice, suddenly developed laryngitis and couldn't sing a note. They have to finish rehearsals by tomorrow night, for the show has to go on Saturday night. In their desperation they called on us to see if we could produce someone who could fill this girl's place."

"I told them that I had just that person. I was thinking of you. I played the recording of your voice, but I didn't tell them that you were not even in town. They might not have been willing to take the risk of waiting for you and they might have looked elsewhere."

She was too surprised to say a word. She was simply stunned. It seemed like a miracle and she had trouble believing that it was true. Her mouth flew open and she exclaimed a subdued "Oh!"

He laughed. "I thought it would take your breath away. I'm so glad for you. If you prove acceptable, it will not only give you a good start, but it will boost your stock with that TV company and they will give us credit for having discovered a star. We'll go right over to the studio and have a talk with the producer."

"Right now?" she gasped. "But I look such a fright. I've had so little sleep and I'm all rumpled from that long ride. Can't I find a reasonable room somewhere, where I can freshen up a bit?"

"If you can do it in a half hour, I'll take you to the place I've engaged for you. You see, I was so sure that you'd be a hit, that I made plans for you."

"Thank you," she murmured. "I hope it won't be too expensive. I don't have money for anything expensive. I'm using my savings to come here and I wasn't planning to stay long. My parents didn't want me to come," she admitted, "so I wouldn't let them pay my way."

"I understand," he said.

Laurie's parents had told him about Beth's family and how they felt about her wanting to follow a musical career.

"Don't bother about expenses just now," he advised. "If you're accepted for the part in that picture, you'll have all that you need, and if you're not, I'll see to it that you're taken care of, for I intend to push the sale of your record which we shall make. That will pay for your trip and then some."

They drove to the place he had engaged for her and she was more surprised when she saw it. She was just a little anxious about the expense, in spite of what he had said. It was an apartment, not just a room.

"Oh, this is lovely!" she exclaimed, "but I'm afraid it's very expensive."

"Just get into your most becoming dress and don't worry about expenses," he said as he sat down to wait for her.

She went into the bedroom and took out one of her prettiest dresses and hastily put it on. She then combed her hair, powdered her face, and returned to the living room.

"Will I do now?" she asked with a smile.

"You'll do just fine," he told her. "Now let's be going. We don't want to be late."

When they reached the studio Beth stared about her with interest. It was much larger than she had thought it would be. On all sides there was noise and movement. Someone was shouting about some scenery in a corner while a musician was idly playing a piano in another set and cameras were being moved about to other locations.

Mr. Marsh, the producer of the number in which Beth was supposed to appear, approached as they entered. Mr. Candler introduced Beth. Marsh gave her a quick appraising glance and he acknowledged the introduction.

"I was afraid you were going to disappoint me," he told Candler.

He turned to Beth and said matter-of-factly, "You're pretty enough for the part, but how much acting experience have you had?"

"Very little," Beth confessed, confused and abashed by the question.

"She has acting ability," Candler told him, "for I've seen her act, though not professionally. But she can sing as well as anyone you have in your employ. I think you'll be convinced when you try her out. I haven't let you down," he added as he saw the bleak look on Marsh's face.

"We'll see," Marsh said and led the way over to a piano. "I'll call one of the musicians to accompany you, if you'll tell him what you want to sing."

"If you don't mind, I'd rather accompany myself," Beth offered.

"All right," he conceded, after a surprised and rather skeptical look.

Beth sat at the piano, and as her fingers ran idly over the keys as she became accustomed to the piano, Marsh's eyes widened. He recognized a talent that was unusual. She began a little lullaby that held infinite pathos and which gave her voice its full measure of touching warmth. When she had finished that, she sang a short aria from an opera.

When she began to sing, those working on other sets stopped and listened. They realized that something unusual was happening. They knew that someone with unusual talent had been discovered. When she finished, there was spontaneous applause.

Beth was surprised and embarrassed at this unexpected outburst, but she managed a smile at her audience before she turned and looked at Marsh.

"You'll do!" he exclaimed. "You bet your life you'll do!" He turned to Candler. "Thank you for bringing us a discovery. If she can act as well as she can play and sing, she has her future made."

He turned back to Beth. "Fortunately the part you will play has very few speaking lines. If you have a good memory and if you can take direction, I'm sure you'll make the grade. But you'll have to learn those lines and the songs you'll be singing by tomorrow morning. We should put you on tonight for rehearsal, but I'll give you a little more time and trust that the rehearsal tomorrow won't have any hitches."

"I'll have to have a piano where I can practice the songs," Beth told him, for she didn't have a piano in her apartment.

"You can practice right here, in one of the soundproof booths," and he led the way to one.

"I'll have to be going," Candler told her. "I'll see you this evening, after I've talked over the terms of your contract."

"But I don't know the way back to the apartment," Beth said, frightened at the thought of being separated from him.

"She's a stranger here," Candler told Marsh. "Send her home in a taxi," and he gave both of them the address of the apartment.

"You put one over on me," Marsh told Candler when they had left Beth. "But I'm glad you did."

Beth was given the music for her two songs and she was soon busy practicing. After an hour or so, she felt reasonably sure that she had memorized both the words and the melody, for she had a quick and retentive memory.

When she had stopped for a while to rest, Marsh came to the booth. He had been listening through an amplifier connected with his office and he was pleased with what he heard. He was glad that the actress who was to have had the part was conveniently incapacitated. This girl was so much better.

"You've learned quickly," he remarked. "Now let's have you sing those two numbers without the music in front of you. And try, while you're singing, to look over the piano at someone standing there who is in love with you, but whom you know you have no right to love. Put all you have in that look, for the camera will be giving you a closeup as you play and sing. The girl who was to play this part couldn't play, so we planned to dub in the notes while she was faking it. We'll have shots taken of your hands as well as your face, so let's see how it will work."

Beth smiled to herself as he gave her the instructions. She had only to think of Gary while she sang, and she knew that she wouldn't be acting. She could see him standing there and looking at her as he had done so many times when she had played for him in the past.

She put her whole soul into the words, while her fingers flew confidently over the keys. Marsh marveled as he watched her.

81

"Where have you been all my life?" he asked, smiling as he repeated the old cliché, when she had finished.

"In college," she replied, answering his smile.

"No college could give you such talent as you have. If you haven't finished college, I'm afraid you won't have time to finish, for if my prediction comes to pass, you'll be too busy to think about college."

He gave her her part of the script and explained the main points of her part of the story.

"Be sure to be letter-perfect when you get here tomorrow morning, because we can't take time for delays or muffing of your part."

"I'll know those lines by tomorrow morning, if I have to stay up all night," she said.

"Good!" he exclaimed. "I'm counting on you."

He led the way outside and called a taxi and gave the driver the address of her apartment. Then he told Beth in an aside that Candler had taken care of the fare.

As she got in and rode to her apartment, her head was in the clouds and her heart was singing a song of delirious joy.

CHAPTER 13

Beth's lines were so few that she soon learned them, but she continued repeating them over and over until she was sure that she could not forget them. She wanted them to come without any effort to remember them for only then could they be spoken naturally. She felt sure that she could put the proper expression in them.

It was late when she finally went to bed and she slept only fitfully, for she wasn't too confident about the music. She was at the studio well ahead of time. Mr. Marsh was already there and he was feeling just a little uncertain about her. If she failed, the play would be in a bad way and the sponsors might cause trouble. He was relieved when Beth arrived early and asked if she might practice more before time to rehearse. She remained in the soundproof booth until she was called for rehearsal.

The set was much smaller then she had anticipated and she marveled at the magic of photography as it flashed these scenes to a viewing public.

Marsh again explained the situation of her part to her and as the rehearsal began, she waited nervously for her scene. When she finally sat at the piano, all her nervousness left her. She had met the young man who was to be her lover in the play. He was also a newcomer, though he had had several successful small parts before. His name was Garth Trammel. He was quite handsome, with brown hair and expressive eyes and an engaging smile. His eyes appraised her quickly when they had been introduced and her heart fluttered as those eyes met hers and she saw approval in them.

When she began to play and to look the part, she felt nervous again as he came and stood on the other side of the piano and looked at her with an adoring glance. The few words he had said before she played the introduction made her still more nervous and she wondered if she could do as well as she had done the day before. It was one thing to sit there and sing to the image of Gary, while her love shone from her eyes, and quite another to look at this stranger with that same expression. She felt timid and inhibited and she had to repeat the scene, so that the director's suggestion that she put more of her heart into that look might be done according to his satisfaction.

Garth smiled at her and gave her a glance that stirred her heart to more fluttering. This time she effaced him entirely and imagined that he was Gary. She succeeded in doing the scene to the satisfaction of the director.

"That's fine," he remarked. "Just do it that way and you'll make your little scene a big one. Try not to think of anything but the man you're in love with, but who cannot marry you because of that wife of his."

She laughed nervously and the others smiled, while Garth remarked in an undertone, "Thank goodness there isn't any wife to keep us apart."

As they waited a moment before repeating the scene just to be sure that it would be perfect, he remarked again, "I want to know you better and I don't have any phantom wife to interfere with our friendship."

"It will be a big relief to know that she isn't somewhere spying on us," Beth replied, and they both laughed.

One of the older members of the cast turned to his companion.

"There goes a budding romance," he observed.

"Let's hope it won't hurt that little girl," his companion replied. "She's sweet and unspoiled. It would be a pity for her to be hurt. That's one sad thing

84

about this profession of ours. It creates romance and then breaks it to shreds. Too many broken hearts."

"You're pessimistic today," the other remarked.

"No, just realistic."

His companion remembered that the other had been the victim of a broken marriage not too long ago. He knew that what his friend had said was true.

When the rehearsal was over, Beth was completely exhausted. They had gone over the whole act often, while the director watched every little detail and made corrections as they went through it.

The other members of the cast were friendly and encouraging, for they knew what a strain Beth was under.

"You'll get used to it is time goes on," the leading girl of the play told her. "It looks so easy and natural on the screen, but the audience doesn't know that it took blood and sometimes tears to make it perfect."

"I can see why it has to be that way," Beth admitted.

She watched Garth in his scene with his screen wife, when he finally told her that he was in love with someone else. As he said this, his eyes wandered an instant to where Beth was, off-stage and watching. She felt guilty of causing trouble when the director saw the glance and cautioned Garth to keep his eyes where they belonged. He made him do the scene over while the others laughed at him and he looked provoked and embarrassed. Beth disappeared until the scene was finished.

"I'm sorry if I bothered you," she told him as he passed her on his way to his dressing room.

"You didn't bother me," he assured her. "I just made a fool of myself because I forgot that wife. I caught a glimpse of you and I couldn't help but take another look. You're enough to make any fellow's eyes wander."

She flushed and did not reply as she turned away. He stopped her.

"Will you go to lunch with me?" he asked. "I'm starved, for it's past two and I didn't have much breakfast."

"Thank you," Beth said. "I'm starved too, for I only had a cup of coffee for my breakfast. I was in a hurry to get down here and practice those songs before time for rehearsal."

"You have a beautiful voice and a wonderful talent," he told her. "You can't blame me for wanting to leave my wife for you," he added with a laugh.

"Thank you," she said with a smile, then seriously, "I wouldn't want that to happen to either of us. It would be terrible, wouldn't it?"

He agreed and in a little while they were ready to leave. He drove them to a restaurant that he knew of.

"This is the first thing I bought with the first money I made," he said, referring to his car. "I had always wanted one, but, of course, couldn't afford it."

"It's beautiful and it just skims along," she commented. "I've always wished that I had a car of my own, but Dad never had enough for me to have one. Our old one is almost worn out. I hope that some day I can buy him a new one."

He asked her about herself and she told him something of her life, her time at college and the fun she had had, and of the ambition that had always consumed her.

"You'll be able to buy your father whatever kind of car he wants," he told her. "After this picture is shown, you'll be getting more offers and I predict you're on your way to the top."

"I do hope that your prediction comes true," she said. "But I also hope that I can finish college. It would break my mother's heart if I didn't do that. She says that I would then be equipped to earn my living, if Dad should die and leave us."

"You won't need to finish college," he assured her. "You'll be making so much more money than you ever could by just teaching and it'll be so much more fun than teaching a lot of unruly kids."

"I hope that will be true," she said, "but I gave up hope for so long that my dream would come true. Even now I can't believe that it may be possible. It all seems like a miracle."

She told him the circumstances that led to her getting this part. He agreed with her that it was like a miracle.

"I wasn't so fortunate," he told her. "I came from a poor family and my parents died when I was still quite young. I hadn't finished high school. I worked at odd jobs, until a talent scout saw me and offered me a chance. I only sing a little, but he saw possibilities in me and I got a start on TV. I'm hoping to go on to parts in motion pictures, for the pay is so much better. I'm glad I got this part, because, if I hadn't, I would never have met you." He gave her a look that brought the color to her face.

"It's nice of you to say that," she told him.

"I'm not just saying it," he said emphatically. "I mean it. You're someone special. I shouldn't be saying this so early in our acquaintance, but it's the truth. I'm not just playing with you. I want your friendship, if that's all you can give me. I'm sure we can have fun together, if you stay on here in New York."

"But I'm not staying on here," she said. "I'm supposed to be on my way home already. I got this part by chance, like I told you. I just came for a few days to make a recording."

"I don't think you'll be going home right away," he maintained. "If you go over as big in this picture as I think you will, they'll keep you on. They'll play you up and after the public sees you in this picture, they'll buy your records and they'll go over big."

"You're very encouraging," she said, "and I hope your prediction comes true, even though I don't know what I'd do if it does. There are my parents to think about. They didn't want me to come here."

They sat there for a while after they had finished eating, then he drove her home and told her that he would pick her up the next day in time for the performance.

She went to the office in her building and made arrangements to send a few telegrams. She sent one to her mother, another to Laurie, and a third one to Gary. She told them on what station and what hour she would be seen. She hoped they would be watching.

When she reached her room, she lay down to rest. She was worn both physically and emotionally. She dozed off and dreamed of Gary, that they were together again and that she was in his arms while he told her that he loved her. She wakened with a start and when she realized that it was only a dream, tears came to her eyes.

She was provoked, yet disturbed by those tears. Why should she be crying over Gary when he made it so clear that they were poles apart and that they could never be any nearer unless she did the one thing that she was farther than ever from doing? How silly she was to be shedding tears over something that could never be, when she was on the eve of her great adventure. She was on a rung of the ladder, even though a very low one, that she could climb until she reached the top as a success.

When the picture was flashed upon the screen and the members of the cast were mentioned, Beth's name was there in big letters, announced as a new discovery.

Three different groups were waiting eagerly for the story to begin. In Beth's home her mother and father sat there tense and excited while she appeared and her voice rang out rich and clear as her fingers ran over the keys. As the director had told her, the camera showed a close-up of her fingers and her lovely profile as well as her full face when her soul-filled eyes rested upon the boy standing on the other side of the piano looking down at her. Her voice rang out beautiful and heart-warming in the touching melody.

Her mother watched her as her own heart thrilled with pride over Beth's loveliness and over her singing and playing, but tears trickled down her cheeks as she realized that this would perhaps be the beginning of something that would take Beth away from her and away from the Lord.

Beth's father sat there silent, but with eyes that were bright with pride. When her scene was finished, he uttered an ejaculation.

"My! But our little one is beautiful! And that voice! I didn't realize how beautiful it was. Aren't you proud of her, honey?"

"Yes, of course I am," she replied, wiping the tears surreptitiously. "Proud, but so afraid."

"Don't be afraid, just trust," he advised as he put an arm around her.

"I'll try," she promised, but her heart was heavy beneath the pride.

Laurie was too excited to sit still until Beth's play came on. When Beth did appear, she uttered a little scream and when the picture was finished, she turned to the others.

"Wasn't she wonderful! Just think! I've discovered a star! If I hadn't introduced her to Mr. Candler, this might never have happened."

In his room alone Gary sat watching the picture. His sister, with whom he lived, had gone out. He had not told her about the picture. He knew it was selfish, but he wanted to be alone as he watched her. When he saw her and heard her voice, his heart ached with longing and the love that he knew to be so futile unless God undertook.

When the picture had faded out, he turned off the set and went to his knees where he prayed that God would keep her from getting farther from him and that, if it was His will, she would one day belong to him.

CHAPTER 14

"You were simply wonderful," Garth told Beth when the last scene had faded and they were alone.

Others had come to her with a word of praise and she was thrilled beyond measure.

"Thank you," she told Garth.

The look she saw in his eyes was something that she had seen many times before in the eyes of other boys, but none of them thrilled her as much.

It was somehow different from the look she had seen in Gary's eyes, but then Gary was different. His eyes had often held that mute expression of a love that was almost adoration and a tenderness that she had never observed in the eyes of any other boy. Just now, however, she was not thinking of Gary. She was wondering about Garth and just what his attitude meant. She found him very attractive and she was flattered by his admiration and his seeming interest in her.

"Is that all you have to say?" he asked teasingly. "Can't you say that I was good all through the play?"

"Of course I can, for you were," she answered with a smile. "I thought you were superb."

"That sounds better," he replied. "But I could never have done as well as I did, if I hadn't caught a glimpse of you off-stage watching me. That gave me the inspiration I needed. When I stood there by that piano and heard you sing while you looked at me with that soul-revealing look, I just wanted to come around that piano and say, 'I'll marry you if I have to get rid of a dozen wives.'"

She laughed, a happy little laugh.

"Let's hope that you won't accumulate a harem."

"If I had you, I'd never want anyone else," he said while his eyes looked into hers with such a possessive light that she lowered her gaze.

She wondered just how much of this he meant and how much was spoken in jest. Or was it what he said to every pretty girl? Perhaps he thought she expected it of him. She didn't credit what he said as the truth.

"Let's stop joking and go and change," she advised. "I'm tired from the strain, but I'm glad that I didn't fumble my part."

"I'm not joking, Beth," he said. "I'm in earnest. I've played around with a few girls, but they, as well as I, knew that it wasn't real. I'm not playing around with you, Beth. The first time I saw you, I knew that you were someone special, the one girl in the world for me. Please believe me when I say that I'm in earnest. I hope that we shall go on to the top together. What do you say to that?"

"I don't know what to say," she told him truthfully. "Please let's go."

"Not before you answer me," he said, blocking the way. "What do you say? What do you think of what I've told you?"

"I just don't know," she repeated. "I can't believe that you're in earnest. I appreciate your friendship, but more than that, there's nothing else that I can say."

"Let's go and have a snack," he suggested. "I'm hungry, for I can't eat just before I go on."

"I'll be glad to go," she agreed. "I'm half-starved and weak as a kitten."

After they had changed and had removed their make-up, they went to the same restaurant they had been to before. He gave their order, then looked at her seriously.

"You don't believe that I'm in earnest," he said. "I know what you're thinking. You're thinking that because you're new in this business, I'm just playing around with you as I have with other girls and that I'm just trying to flatter you and build up your ego, to amuse myself. Isn't that true?"

"I don't know what to think," she said honestly. "Perhaps I was thinking that. You don't look like that kind of a person, but then," and she gave him a little smile, "I've never met that kind of a person. I like you and I would like to have you for a friend, but I never thought that you were serious. We've known each other such a short time."

"I know that, but will you believe me if I tell you that I am serious?" he asked anxiously.

"I'll try to," she promised, "but I find it hard to believe that what you have said really comes from your heart, so let's not argue about it, but just have a pleasant time together."

"But I insist that I am in earnest, even if we have known each other such a short time. Will you believe me when I tell you that I love you? I fell in love with you that very first morning. I know that it sounds silly and impossible, but it's true. Will you try to believe me?"

"Yes, if you really want me to," she replied while her heart fluttered strangely. This was something that seemed so utterly impossible, yet it thrilled her with a new thrill, for it was such a strange, fantastic approach to love.

Her love for Gary and their love for each other was something that had grown with the years. It was dear and had been deep within her heart, but there had been no romantic thrill to a new sensation, for it had seemed to be there always.

This was something that had sprung into being so suddenly that it was fantastic and romantic in the extreme.

"Can't you say that you do care a little for me?" His voice was low and begging and his eyes were pleading as they looked into hers.

"I can't say any more that I've already said," she told him. "I like you, but I've never thought about loving you. I haven't known you long enough and I just took it for granted that you had a sweetheart some-where. I've never had time even to think about love. I was too busy thinking about doing my part perfectly."

"But you will think about it now?" he persisted. "I know I sound like a silly kid, but I can't help that. I want your love, Beth, and I'm asking you to think about loving me, so do try, won't you?"

"I'll think about it," she promised as their order came and they talked of other things.

When they reached her apartment, he took her to her door and as he told her good night, he attempted to kiss her. She drew away. She wasn't ready for that. She couldn't believe, even yet, that he was in earnest. Even if he was, she wasn't in love with him and she didn't want his kiss unless she was.

"Sorry," he apologized. "You're just not like other girls. Most of them expect it. Maybe that's why I love you, because you are different."

When she had closed the door to her apartment, she stood there for a while in the darkness and suddenly her thoughts turned to Gary. How tender and respect-ful he had been! He had waited so long before he had dared to kiss her and then it was only when he knew that she was willing. How different he was from this exciting young man who was so sure of himself and so sure of her response to the love he had declared for her.

A sudden wave of homesickness swept over her and the longing to see Gary, to have him hold her in his arms and kiss her, the longing to feel his heart beat against hers as he held her with his cheek against hers.

She was glad that she would be going home in a day or so. She had had her first taste of fame, but she was willing to forego a further taste until later. She would be willing to return to college in the fall and finish her education before trying further flights up the ladder of fame.

The next morning she received a phone call from Mr. Candler. She had forgotten that she was to make a record.

"Congratulations," he said. "You were just perfect. You acted like a professional and your voice was really something unusual. Marsh phoned me last night right after the show and he gave me permission to make a recording of the two songs you sang in the show. He thinks I've given him a real discovery. When you come over, I'll have your check waiting for you. Then we'll get ready for that recording."

When she hung up the phone her heart was racing wildly again. Gone were thoughts of returning home, gone the homesickness, forgotten was the longing to see Gary and to be held in his arms. Fame again beckoned to her. That recording would have advertising of her part in the picture. She didn't know what the future held, but she realized that it would probably be some time before she would return home. Gone also were thoughts of college.

She had forgotten all about the check that was due her. She didn't even speculate about the amount. Her only thought was that she had succeeded on the first rung of the ladder toward fame and that further success would lure on to further climbing.

When she reached the studio, Mr. Candler greeted her with a smile.

"You've hit the jackpot," he said. "Marsh sent over a reporter from one of the TV magazines for an interview. She is waiting outside. Your recording can wait until she has finished her interview. The fact that you are on for a recording by my company will give you an added boost in her article."

Beth's eyes were glowing and her heart was beating wildly with excitement as she met the reporter. She was a young, attractive woman and Beth at once felt at ease when they sat down together and began to talk. Beth noticed that there was a photographer there also.

When the reporter questioned her, she told her frank-

94

ly of her lifelong ambition to become a concert singer and how she had had this first chance on TV.

"What you did in the picture, certainly proved that you have both talent and ability to act," the young woman told her.

When the interview was ended the photographer took several shots of her.

"We'll do our best for you," the reporter said. "Perhaps before long you may be on the front page of one of our issues."

"That would be wonderful," Beth replied, and thanked the reporter for her good wishes as they both left.

When Beth returned to Candler's office, her head was swimming.

"I'm so overcome that I'm really dizzy," she told him. "I still can't believe that this is all real."

"It's real, to be sure," Candler said with an amused smile. "Your head may be swimming still more when this record hits the market. Just the announcement that it is from the picture Double Trouble will give it a boost. Remember that there were thousands watching you last night, for that show is one of the most popular ones on the networks."

"I'm supposed to go home in a day or so," she said. "Mother has been expecting me before now."

"Let's not discuss that now," he advised. "Let's get down to business with those recordings. By the way, here's your check. I hope it pleases you."

When she saw the amount, her eyes flew open and she uttered a little gasp.

"Pleased?" he asked.

"Pleased!" she exclaimed. "I'm simply overwhelmed. I never dreamed it would be this much. I never had this much money in my life. Why, this is more than Dad makes in a month of hard work."

"There'll be more when this record hits the market," he assured her.

The dream seemed about to come true. Everything else was forgotten but that tremendous prospect.

95

If she could have looked into the future, she might even have refused to make that recording. She might have been willing to turn her back on the hope of fame and success and have fled home on the first plane. But she couldn't look into the future and she had failed to heed the whisper of conscience. She could see only the present and that present was bright with the light of a single star, the star of success, wealth and joy undreamed of.

CHAPTER 15

After the thrill of her first success and the interview and the recording had died down, Beth began to feel the reaction which usually comes after such an experience and she began to be homesick again. Though she had been assured of other parts, they had not come and she found time hanging on her hands. The only friend she had was Garth and he was away on location for another picture.

She told Mr. Candler that she thought she would go home for a little visit. She had written to her mother and to Laurie, telling them all that had happened and her mother had answered her letter. She shed a few tears as she read her mother's letter, for, though it sounded cheerful and she told how glad she was that Beth was happy in her success, when she read the last few lines, she could read the heartache in them that didn't appear in her other news.

"I miss you terribly, honey," her mother wrote. "I hate to go into your room to clean it, but I want you to be happy in the way you have chosen and I pray for you every day that God will take care of you and lead you in the right path. Your room is waiting for you whenever you want to come back. I pray that it will be soon."

Beth saw the faint mark of a tear splash at the bottom of the sheet and she knew that her mother had shed tears while she finished the letter. Just then she wanted more than anything to see her mother and to be held in her arms as she had been when she was a little child.

When she told Mr. Candler of her intention, he objected strenuously.

"You can't leave town now," he told her. "The very moment you leave here, there may be a call for you to appear in another picture and if you're not right on the spot, you'll lose another chance. Just remember that directors have short memories and if they can't get you, they'll find someone else just as they found you. There are too many other talented young girls waiting for the chance that came to you."

"But I'm so homesick," she confessed. "I'm lonely here with so little to do."

"That's one of the sacrifices that you will have to make, if you want a career. Actors are often far from where they would like to be, but if they want to carry on, they have to go where they're sent. If you have nothing to do, suppose you enroll in the Major School of acting. You'll need more experience than you have and this will be a fine opportunity to put your idle time to good use."

"Isn't that terribly expensive?" she asked. "I'm afraid my money won't hold out if I have to wait around very long for another part."

"Don't worry about that," he advised. "I'll get a good agent for you. I'm not really an agent, you understand, just a go-between for that first offer. I'm so sure that you'll be a success, that I'm willing to stake you if your funds don't hold out until you get another call."

She reluctantly consented to give up the idea of going home so Candler phoned the Major School and made an appointment for her. She knew that she needed training and she entered into her work with enthusiasm and the determination to make the most of her opportunity.

Weeks passed and she heard nothing from the TV company nor did she get any news about her record. She was beginning to despair when suddenly a call came for her to be in another picture. Her spirits rose and she was happy again while her longing to see her mother was forgotten.

Her record was beginning to sell. With the good review she had had from the critics in the television magazine and in some papers, people were interested in buying the records. Her picture and brief history on the cover of her record helped in the sale. Mr. Candler had done everything possible to help the sale. He recognized the possibilities for himself if she succeeded and if her record became a best-seller.

He had engaged an agent for her and the agent had succeeded in getting her this call.

When she prepared to go on location in the mountains of New Hampshire, she was surprised and pleased to know that Garth was in the cast. He was to play opposite her again. He had just returned from a successful part in that other production and the director of this picture remembered what a hit they had made together in Beth's first picture. Garth had not had time to contact Beth before he made preparations to leave with the others in the cast.

"What a break!" he told her when they met before take-off. "I didn't know until just before we were ready to leave who was the one I was to play opposite."

"I'm glad we'll be together again," Beth told him. "It'll be easier working with someone I know than with a stranger. I was beginning to be nervous again."

"I'll be more than your partner," he said, referring to the script. "I'll be your very own lover-boy and in the end we'll fade out together, to live happily ever after."

Beth remembered the script and she knew that there would be several love scenes between them. Though they didn't have the leads in the story, they did have important parts. She didn't reply, but her heart beat happily as she saw his eyes and thought of what would take place in the scenes.

One of the scenes was in a moonlit spot on the slope of a mountain when he had just rescued her from a fall which might have injured her or possibly killed her. He took her in his arms and whispered "This is for real," so low that the mikes couldn't hear the words. Then he kissed her.

She was thrilled at the touch of his lips, but the presence of the camera crew embarrassed her and she unconsciously drew away from Garth as she saw them. She should have been looking at Garth.

The director caught the unconscious act and the wandering glance. He stopped the act and approached them. She had ruined the scene and he was cross.

"Young lady," he snapped. "You're supposed to be in love with this young man. You're supposed to be looking at him and not casting an eye at the camera crew. Even if you hate the sight of him, pretend that you adore him. Make that kiss a delight, not a torture."

"But I don't hate him!" Beth cried, embarrassed and frightened.

"Then pretend that you love him and kiss him as if you did. That first attempt was a terrible dud. Haven't you ever been kissed before?" he asked with a hint of a smile.

"Y-e-s," Beth stammered, "but not while a crew was watching me."

"Then don't act as if you never have been and forget the crew. All they're interested in is getting this scene in the can and going home."

This time she really tried and her heart began that wild fluttering as Garth's lips clung to hers and he held her so close that she could scarcely breathe.

"Good!" the director exclaimed. "Now come slowly toward the camera and look at lover-boy with your heart in that look."

She tried to obey. Garth's eyes held what the director wanted and she wondered if they spoke the truth. She was glad when the scene was finished and the director was satisfied.

When the picture was finally finished and they were

preparing for the return journey, Garth had a little while with her before they had to join the others.

"I can't believe that a beautiful girl as you are has never been kissed before. At least you acted in that scene as if you never had. Why did you pull away from me?"

"Because I was embarrassed by that crew watching me. I'm not used to kissing in public. I just forgot that I was acting and I couldn't act the part because I didn't feel what I was supposed to feel."

"That means that you're not the least bit in love with me, doesn't it?" he asked, disappointed. "I was hoping that you might be, just a little bit."

"No, I'm not," she admitted. "I couldn't get used to kissing someone I didn't love."

"You mean that you've never kissed a boy you didn't love?" he asked doubtfully.

She nodded. She wished he would change the subject.

"Then you have been in love with someone, for you told the director that you have been kissed," he remarked.

"That is my own private affair," she replied. "Please drop the subject. I'm tired of this questionnaire."

"I was only trying to find out something because I love you," he said. "I wonder if the reason you can't love me is that you still love this other boy you left when you came here. I believe you do, Beth. I'm not trying to probe into your private affairs, but it means so much to me. If you still love him, then I know I don't have a chance. But if you do love him, I wonder why you consented to leave him to some other girl. I know I wouldn't want to leave you, if you ever loved me. Would you tell me why you left him? Is there any hope for me?"

"I left him because I wanted a career and he had different ideas about life. We could never be reconciled to each other's viewpoints."

"What were those viewpoints?"

"He's a Christian and I'm not. He wanted me to give

101

up the thought of a career and become a Christian, but I couldn't see it that way. I want to live my life and get all the joy out of it while I'm still young. Later on, perhaps, I may see things differently."

"What do you mean by being a Christian?" he asked. "We're all Christians, unless we're heathen and I know I'm not a heathen. I believe in God. I don't drink or carouse around. I try to be a pretty decent fellow. I'm like you. I want a career and I intend to have it if it's possible. Just what do you mean by being a Christian?" he repeated.

"A real Christian is one who knows that he's a sinner because all of us are. We have a sinful nature which we inherited from Adam. That person, because he knows he's a sinner, comes to God and asks Him to forgive him and to save his soul, through Jesus Christ. When a person does that, then God forgives him and he is given salvation and eternal life. That doesn't mean that he can go on sinning again. His whole life is turned over to God so that He can have full control of that life."

"I never heard that before," he acknowledged. "A Christian must be a pretty dull and unhappy person. If he can't do the things he wants to do, what's the use of living? What's life for, if not to have a good time and make the most of it?"

"It's given to a person to prepare for eternity," she said, becoming more serious as she heard her own words.

"Now you're trying to frighten me," he said with a little laugh. "Dying is something that I never think about. It's too frightening. Why bother about it until it comes?"

"But you never know when it's coming. My mother is a Christian. She's a wonderful person and is as happy as anyone could be. She tried to teach me and to make me accept what she taught, that our main purpose in life is to do as much as we can to win souls of others who don't love the Lord and who haven't yielded their heart and life to Him."

"If what she taught you is true, then why didn't you do what she wanted you to do? Why couldn't you do what the boy you loved wanted you to?"

"Because I just didn't want to," she confessed. "I wanted to have a career, like I said, while I'm young and able to enjoy a career."

"But, as you say, you may never know when death may come. And you're not ready to meet it if what you say is true."

"I know it." A note of sadness crept into her voice. "But, like you, I don't want to think about it. I just hope it won't come before I'm ready for it."

"You'd better mend your ways and get ready for it," he said lightly. Dismissing the subject and taking her hand, he led her to where their car was waiting to take them to the airport.

On the short flight to the city, they were both rather silent. They were thinking of their conversation and she was vaguely disturbed by what she had said, something she had never discussed before with anyone except Gary and her mother. She was thinking how often her mother had tried to make her think seriously of what she was saying and how she had rebelled and had refused to think about it. She was afraid that if she did, she might yield to her mother's persuasions and that would spoil her dream of ambition.

Garth didn't mention the scene in the picture again, nor did he repeat a word of the love he had professed before he had gone away. He also was thinking of what Beth had said, things that were new and strange to him.

Beth wondered if Garth had really meant what he had said when he told her that he loved her, even though he had repeated it once in the conversation about that kiss on the mountain side. But that could have been only his excuse for his further questions. She wondered what she would say and how she would react, if he really meant the love he professed. She thought of that scene on the mountainside and as she did so, there came again that warm little flutter of her heart at the clinging touch of his lips.

The memory of Gary and his tender kiss had faded from her thoughts. There was no longer a longing in her heart for the touch of his lips.

CHAPTER 16

The days again began to pass monotonously and Beth became discouraged and discontented and homesick, as no more calls came. She was almost willing to give up her hope of becoming a success as a musician.

In the few parts she had had, there had been no opportunity to display her voice and she was not satisfied to become just a bit performer. That was not what she had come to New York for. It was her hope to become a concert singer.

The record upon which she had counted to help her in her effort to succeed was not selling as well as it had given promise in the beginning. There were too many others who were well-known to the public and they passed her record by after the first rush of sales. She began to understand that it was not so much talent that counted in this "rat race" as it was popularity, and how could she become popular if she were never given a chance to display her talents to the public?

She told her agent as much and that she had about decided to go home and forget the whole thing. He persuaded her to carry on a while longer, assuring her that a break would come, if she would only be patient.

When she thought of the drab life she would be leading there and of the heartache that would be hers with the knowledge that she had failed, she decided to take her agent's advice and stick it out a while longer.

Just when her funds were running low and she knew that she would have to go home if she didn't get a call soon, she would receive a bit part that paid very little in comparison to what she had expected and which gave her no opportunity to sing or play. She took it out of desperation. She didn't realize that the director was using her beauty to give more interest to the picture, and that he was not interested in using an unknown in a more important part which would be a risk. He had many seasoned and talented players whose names were well-known and who would be no risk to the picture.

She only saw Garth at infrequent intervals. He was in increasing demand for more important parts. He was fast rising to the top and that made Beth more unhappy than ever. They never had another opportunity to play opposite each other and that made her more despondent. She felt that he was growing away from her.

When they were together in those brief intervals, he was engrossed with his work and that was all he could talk about. The only sign he showed that he still cared, was his good-night kiss when they parted, with perhaps an occasional word of endearment.

She had reached the point where she waited eagerly and hopefully for that kiss. She began to wonder if he was afraid to become involved with her, since he was on his way to the top — that he wanted to be free from any ties with her.

She knew that he was constantly in contact with girls as pretty as she was and she feared that he would fall in love with one of them. If that should happen, she knew that she would be desolate indeed, with her one reason for remaining and struggling over disappointment taken from her.

She sometimes wondered if she loved him or if it were only infatuation, or if he was just someone to whom she could cling in her loneliness. She knew that she thrilled to his kiss and the fact that he had showed her such marked attention from the beginning flattered her. He was very handsome and she had seen the way other girls cast admiring eyes at him when they had played in the same picture.

When time began to drag heavily upon her and her

hopes had reached their lowest ebb, she received a call from her agent telling her that he had at last landed a good part for her. He told her that she would have a chance to sing and also to play the piano. He seemed quite enthusiastic about the part and her spirits rose, though his first news left her cold. She had reached the place where nothing seemed to enthuse her.

The agent didn't tell her that he had very little to do with her getting the part. The girl who had been selected to play the part had married quite suddenly and had left on a honeymoon with a nonprofessional. The director had phoned Candler and asked about Beth. Candler put him in touch with Beth's agent.

When Beth met the director, Mr. Kennedy, and she had an opportunity to read the script, her spirits really soared. Her part was an important one and she would have the opportunity to play and sing, as her agent had told her.

She tried out for the part and both Kennedy and the others of the crew were pleased with what she had done. She was glad that, even when she was most disconsolate, she had continued her studies at the school of acting. She immediately went to rehearsal for the first few scenes. The greater part of the story would be filmed in California.

A few days after she had begun rehearsal, she received a letter from her father. She had not written home in some time, for she was too discouraged to write. Her father seldom wrote and she wondered why he was writing now.

As she opened the envelope, a sense of dread crept over her and she took the letter out with fingers that trembled. She was not mistaken, for as she began to read, her heart sank.

"Honey," her father began, "I hate to write to you like this, but I'm just a little worried about your mother. She hasn't been feeling well for some time, but she wouldn't let you know how bad off she was, because she didn't want to worry you. She's missed you so much that she just seemed to pine away. She tried to be cheerful and not let me see how her heart ached for a sight of you. Now she's down in bed and I'm really worried about her. The doctor doesn't say much, but I'm afraid there is something seriously wrong with her. He said that if she doesn't respond to the medicine, he'll have to have her at the hospital for tests. I just couldn't ask him what he thought the trouble was, because I was afraid to know. I believe that if you could run down home for a little visit, it would cheer her up and she would get better. I miss you, honey. Please come if you can."

She put the letter down while tears filled her eyes. She was having the old struggle between love and ambition and, after a time of tears and heartache, ambition won again.

She wrote her father and sent it by air mail.

"Dear Dad," she wrote. "I want more than anything to come down and see you and Mom, but I've just had the biggest break of my career. It's the answer to all my dreams and hopes. If I come now, I'll lose the one great opportunity of my life, for if I drop out of the cast now, I'll never get another chance like this. I'm on contract for this picture and I dare not break it.

"As soon as I've finished the picture, I'll fly down and see you both. I'll just pray that Mom will be better. Tell her that I love her more than anyone else in the world and next to her, I love you."

Her heart was heavy as she mailed the letter, but she was so intent upon thoughts of her rehearsal the next day and the night trip to California that she tried to forget what her father had written.

When her father read the letter there was a hard light in his eyes and a grim expression upon his face. He tore the letter to shreds and didn't let his wife know that he had written or received an answer.

Beth was so excited over her trip to California and her part in the play, that her brief sorrow over her mother's condition was pushed into the background of her thoughts.

The rehearsals took longer than she thought, for this picture was to be a special feature and it would take an hour to produce.

Beth was to play the part of a young opera singer who had gotten her first break because of the temperamental outburst of the one who was to have played the part. She had left the scene after an argument with the director and had refused to go on with the part. She had been singing in a night club when she had been spotted by the director, after the argument with the other actress. He had given her a test in desperation, and she had been given the part.

It reminded Beth of her first chance on TV, for the circumstances had been somewhat similar.

When the rehearsals were over and the picture had been made, all of the working crew were enthusiastic over Beth's performance. She had had both the opportunity to sing and to play the piano, which she did in the night club scene.

When she watched the runoff of the film, she could scarcely believe that she was looking at herself. She was satisfied that she had done well and was happy over the outcome of her efforts. She was guaranteed a contract and this made her even more happy as she took the plane back to New York.

It was not until she was on her way to her apartment that she began to think of her mother and her father's letter. She must take time out for a weekend visit, if no more, to see them both. She hoped that her mother was better. Perhaps Dad had exaggerated her condition, not purposely, but because he was so worried about her. She would tell them about her picture and the trip and they would understand why she couldn't have come sooner.

When she opened the door of her apartment, she saw two telegrams that had been slipped through the letter slot on her door. Her heart skipped a beat as she picked them up and she stood there a moment with them in her hands, afraid to open them.

The first one she opened bore the date of a few days after she had left for California. It contained only a few words. "Your mother is dying. Come at once. Dad."

She opened the other with hands that trembled, for she felt that she knew the worst. It shocked her even more than the first one had done. It was signed by Laurie's father and read, "Your father died of a heart attack at your mother's funeral. Let us know what we should do, if you can't come."

She dropped into a chair, stunned and shocked and heart-broken. Both gone while she was having the time of her life fulfilling her ambition. It was quite a while before she could cry. She was too stunned for tears. When she did begin, the flood came and she sobbed hysterically.

The glitter of fame seemed a tarnished, useless bauble that had become a thing that brought torture at the thought of it. The call of ambition seemed like some tantalizing demon that had led her on with false hopes, knowing all the while that she would reach the edge of an abyss.

Why, oh why had she not gone when her father had asked her to come? She would have missed this chance, but there would not have been the rebuke of conscience which she felt she would carry all the rest of her life.

What was there in life now, when there was no one who loved her? What would the world care that her heart was crushed and that guilt weighed so heavily upon her that she felt she couldn't go on with life?

What would fortune or fame amount to when there was no one to share it, no one to be proud of her even if they didn't agree with the course she had chosen?

She had forgotten Laurie's letter lying in her lap. She had picked it up with the telegrams. When she had managed to control her weeping, and the agony that went with the tears, she opened the letter.

Laurie gave her the details of the tragedy. She told her that her mother had not been well for quite some time before she would consent to have the doctor call. When they finally took her to the hospital, she was practically dying and there was no hope for her. Laurie didn't know the nature of the disease, but she said that Beth's father had been beside her day and night until the end came.

The doctor told them that her father had had some heart condition, but that he didn't want his wife to know about it, because he didn't want her to worry about it while she was so sad over Beth's being away. He had tried to get additional insurance, but he had been denied. Just as they were leaving the cemetery, he collapsed and died a few hours later.

"We wish you would come home," Laurie continued. "We tried to reach you, but we couldn't find out where you were. You never gave your father your address where you were going for the picture. Your father was so distressed when he couldn't get an answer to his telegram and we were so worried because we didn't get an answer to the one Dad sent you. Please let us know what to do, for there is no one to take care of the expenses and there are plenty. No one knows what to do, for there is no one to take over your father's estate except you. I surely do feel sorry about all this, honey, and my heart aches for you, but do come home as soon as you get this letter."

Beth let the letter drop to the floor while tears rolled down her face unheeded. She dreaded the thought of going back to that empty house, but she knew that those bills had to be paid, for her father would feel terrible if he knew about them. He had always been so punctual about paying his bills.

Finally she got up and went wearily to bathe her face. It was time for her to eat, but she wasn't hungry. She was weak and shaky, but she knew that she would have to keep her strength for what lay ahead, so she went downstairs and forced some food down. Then she phoned her agent and told him what had happened and that she was leaving as soon as she could get transportation. She was thankful that she had been paid part of her salary while they were on location, an advance on her pay for the picture. She went to the bank and deposited the check, then she phoned the plane ticket office and engaged a seat on an early flight.

She dreaded the trip so that she was tense and nervous and on the verge of collapse.

When she reached the house, she realized that she didn't have a key. She was sure that Laurie's father must have a key, so she went to the nearest phone and called Laurie. Laurie said that they did have the key and that she would bring it over at once.

When she came, she said nothing, but just took Beth in her arms and held her close while they cried together.

Finally Beth sobbed, "I didn't know about anything until I came home and found the telegrams and your letter. I never thought to send Dad my address, though even so, it might not have reached me, if he had wired me, for we were way out in the country. Please don't think that I didn't care. I couldn't believe that Mother was as bad as he said she was. I thought he was just worried."

"I understand," Laurie assured her as she hugged Beth tighter. "I know how you feel and I wish there was something that I could do to help."

"Would you mind if I'd rather go in alone?" Beth asked.

"Oh course not. I understand," Laurie assured her. "I'll be ready any time you need me. We want you to come over and have dinner with us this evening. Please come."

"Thanks, but I couldn't eat a bite," and Beth's lip trembled. "I don't think I can face anyone just now. Give me a little time. I'll get along all right. I've got to face this alone, but I'll try to get the strength to do it. I'll call you when I'm able to talk about it, but I can't just now. I know I'll need your father's help."

112

"Dad will be glad to do anything he can," Laurie told her. "Let me know when you want me to come over and I'll be right here. I'm glad school is out and won't keep me from coming whenever you call."

Laurie kissed her and left her. Beth remembered that Laurie had graduated. The thought brought added pain. If she hadn't gone off, following the glittering will-of-the-wisp of fame, they would have graduated together. Now she had neither fame nor loved ones, nor the finished education to which she had looked forward with such eagerness. That now seemed ages past.

She unlocked the door and entered the empty, desolate house that had once been a home and such a happy one. Now it was just an empty shell, filled with memories that tortured her as she looked around and saw the keepsakes and the little treasures that her mother had kept so carefully.

Voices seemed to call out to her, voices that were accusing, voices that tore at her heart as they seemed to say, *You left all this and the love that would have held you and tried to make you happy — for what? What does anything matter, now that you are alone? What does life matter? It will never be the same. You can't undo the past and you can never forget that you threw away a love that can never have an equal, when you could have given your love and your companionship to those who adored you.*

"Oh, shut up! Shut up!" she cried as she put her hands over her ears to shut out those accusing voices that seemed so real. She knew that it was only the voice of her conscience accusing her and warning her that as long as she lived they would be there. She could never get away from them.

She dropped to the floor, then fell upon her face and sobbed, bitter, heart-tearing sobs that lasted until she was too weak to sob.

CHAPTER 17

Beth lost track of time as she lay there sobbing. When the racking sobs finally ceased, she continued to cry quietly while thoughts of her happy childhood scenes moved by in memory. There was the time when she had brought her puppy into the living room and the puppy had knocked over a vase, that her mother prized highly, from the coffee table. Instead of scolding her or spanking her for disobeying by bringing the puppy into that room, she had put the puppy out and had taken the now weeping child and set her down while she had patiently explained that disobedience was a sin and that it made God sorry. Then she had told Beth that she would have to pay the penalty for her disobedience. She wouldn't be allowed to attend the little birthday party of a friend, something that she had been looking forward to eagerly.

Tears and pleading didn't alter the verdict of that penalty. It left such a lasting impression upon her that she seldom disobeyed again.

Other events passed before her in memory until at last there came the scene at the station when she had had the last sight of her mother. She knew that she would never forget the look on her mother's face as she said those last few words, trying to hide her sorrow because the child she loved so much was leaving her to go out into a world of which she did not approve.

With this last scene in memory, the tears started again and she continued crying until she was startled by the ringing of the doorbell. Laurie was there with a tray in her hands while her father waited in the car.

"Mother was sure that you would be able to eat a little something when you had had time to rest, so she sent you some of our dinner," Laurie said.

She appeared not to notice Beth's tear-stained face, for she didn't want to start the tears again.

"Thank your mother for her sweet thoughtfulness," Beth said through lips that trembled. "And thank you and your father for bringing it. I know I shall enjoy it when I'm able to eat."

Laurie gave her a swift kiss upon her wet cheek and there were tears in her own eyes, for she knew that Beth must be suffering from grief and remorse.

Beth made her way wearily to the kitchen. She felt as if she were walking in some horrible dream, that this couldn't really be true. She couldn't believe that it was real, that she was alone in an empty house that had always been so full of happiness. As she remembered how her father had always had a little joke to tell when they sat at a meal, sobs again choked her, but she stifled them. She would have to try to control her feelings, for she couldn't go on like this. She would break under the strain and there was so much to do.

She put the tray down, thinking she would come back to it later and warm the food when she felt that she could swallow it. She carried her suitcase up to her room and stood in the doorway looking around at the familiar scene. It was just as she had left it, with all of her little trinkets just where she had put them. She knew that her mother had kept this room scrupulously clean and she knew that she had prayed constantly that Beth would someday come back to it, never to wander from it again.

A sigh from her tortured heart escaped her as she put the suitcase down and prepared to hang up the few dresses that she had brought. She returned to the kitchen and warmed the delicious food that Laurie had

115

brought, but she had no appetite and after toying with the food for a while, she gave up the attempt to eat.

It was a terrible ordeal for her to sleep in this silent, empty house that was no longer a home, but which was filled with so many poignant memories. Voices from the past continued to call to her as she tossed to and fro and slept only in snatches.

The next morning she phoned Laurie's father and asked him what she should do and just how she could go about settling her father's estate.

He offered to take her to his lawyer, so she went with him. The lawyer, Mr. Edwards, was kind and sympathetic. Laurie's father had already given him the facts in the case. The first thing they did was to go to the bank and receive permission to open the box where her father had his papers.

There was little in the box beside her father's insurance papers and a book that contained the record of a small savings account. She knew that her father had had a struggle to save the little that was there.

When the bill from the hospital came and those from the funeral home, Beth was faced with the appalling fact that there was not enough money to meet those bills.

She told the lawyer that she would have to sell the house to meet these expenses and he said he would make arrangements with an agent to try to sell the property.

When she returned to the house which would soon belong to some stranger, she was past weeping. She was determined to try to keep from crying, for tears would only unnerve her and she would have to keep her strength until everything was settled and she could leave the town which she had called home, but which she never wanted to see again.

Painful memories would be the only things that would be left and she didn't want to have to face those memories again.

She had an offer for the house sooner than she had hoped and since the offer was a fair one, she was advised to take it.

While the furniture was being disposed of, she received a letter from her agent urging her to return as soon as possible. He didn't want to lose such a good prospect for stardom, for when Beth's picture was released it received very good reviews in the TV magazines and her stock was rising. He enclosed some of the newspaper clippings in his letter which were also quite favorable and gave her a good mention as a promising young starlet.

He said that he had her contract waiting for her to sign, for the director of her picture had kept his promise and gave her one which was quite satisfactory to the agent.

She read the letter with little interest and put the clippings aside without even reading them. She would have been thrilled a short time ago, before tragedy had laid its heavy hand upon her, but now it meant nothing to her.

She knew, she realized dully, that she would have to keep on working, for she had no other means of support outside the field she had chosen.

When the last of the furniture had been disposed of and the final act of sale had been passed, Laurie urged her to stay with her until she left town. She couldn't refuse Laurie's pleading, for she felt that this might be the last time she would see Laurie.

They had little to say as they undressed and got into bed together. Beth remembered how they had giggled and talked far into the night when they were youngsters and had spent the night with each other. Now it was so different. She couldn't talk, for she choked at the memory of the happy times in the past and Laurie was afraid to talk, for fear that she would say something that would start the tears again. But she did put her arms around Beth before they tried to go to sleep and murmured, "Honey, just remember that my heart aches with yours. I've always loved you and I always shall. Never forget that. If you ever need a friend, I'll always be at hand to help you in any way I can."

"Thanks," Beth murmured. "I love you too. You're the only one left who really cares. I'll never forget you, no matter what happens, even if I never get to see you again."

"You'll be able to come back someday when the pain has lessened," Laurie told her.

"It'll never lessen," Beth said as a sob shook her.

She stifled it and tried to go to sleep, but sleep wouldn't come.

When at last everything had been taken care of and all the bills had been paid, there was just a pittance left for Beth, but she didn't care. Nothing mattered now, but the fact that she would have to go on living when she'd just rather end it all and go out into forgetfulness. However, she know only too well that there never could be forgetfulness. Her mother had taught her that she couldn't forget, for life never ended. The soul went out into eternity either to be with Christ or forever separated from Him in endless punishment.

She gave Laurie a tearful good-by as she left the town she never wanted to see again. Laurie urged her, through tears, to write to her, but Beth didn't promise. She was past talking.

When she boarded the plane and flew into the darkness, there seemed no hope of light ahead. The morning would not bring back the light of happiness and enthusiasm over a career for which she now had no ambition to follow. Life would be drab and every memory would bring reproach and pain.

The memory of her father's letter brought a sudden stab of torture. If she had only answered his pleading and had gone home! If she had only let that one big chance slip while she went home to the mother who was dying without her presence to comfort her in her loneliness, she would be free from this agonizing reproach which she felt would never leave her.

What would success or ambition fulfilled mean now? There would be no one to care, no one to be proud of her even though the career she had chosen was so far from what they had wanted for her. Success would be the tasteless fruit which gave no pleasure in its consumption.

CHAPTER 18

The little apartment that had seemed so luxurious to Beth when she had first occupied it, now seemed drab and crammed. The memory of the roomy cottage that was no longer hers, made it seem more drab and dreary than ever. Tears filled her eyes as she shut the door and looked about her. The thought that she now had no other home, that she could never go back to the old place again, brought them streaming down her face.

Until now, she had always had the assurance that one day she would be able to go home for a visit. Whenever homesickness had assailed her, she had struggled on just a little longer, knowing that when success finally came, she could return home and bask in that success, sure that her parents would love her and be proud of her, even though they didn't approve of what she was doing.

Now there was just an empty house with strangers who would soon be occupying it. Laurie would soon forget her when time passed and they didn't see each other again. She would be marrying Bob before long. Beth was sure of that. She would be out of Laurie's life completely.

The thought of marriage brought thoughts of Garth. She had not thought of him since she had read those telegrams. Now she wondered dully where he was and if he still thought of her, if he did really love her. Just now, she didn't care. Nothing mattered and she didn't care what happened.

She would have to go on living, but she wondered

how long she could keep going on in her profession when the goal of ambition was no longer there. There was nothing but pain and sorrow and remorse.

When she had unpacked her clothes and had rested for a little while, she realized that she was hungry. It had been so long since she had eaten a full meal. She went downstairs and ordered a meal and tried to eat it with relish, but she had to force the food down because she knew that she would have to keep her strength.

She remembered that her agent had said that there would be another part for her in the near future and she thought that she had better phone him and let him know that she had returned. Parts came seldom and she had so little on hand, even with what was left of her father's estate.

When the agent answered her call, he was not too pleasant.

"You've lost your chance for another good part," he told her. "Why did you stay so long? Marsh was disappointed when he tried to get you. You may lose your contract if you disappear this way and don't get in touch with him."

"I don't care what he thinks or how he feels," Beth retorted, angry and hurt that he showed so little sympathy for her grief. "If he wants to cancel the contract, then let him. My mother and father died while I was away on location for that last picture. How could he expect me to come at his call? I don't care what happens," she ended as her voice choked.

"I'm sorry," he said in more sympathetic tones. "I'll explain to Marsh. He may have something for you before long. Don't feel that you don't care. That's not the way to feel when you're a young ambitious player. Be eager to get whatever comes your way."

"I'm not ambitious any longer," she told him. "I'll have to keep on working, but I'm no longer ambitious."

He gave her a few encouraging words, promising to let her know as soon as he heard anything, then she hung up. There was nothing to do but wait and waiting was torture. She wanted to be kept busy, if only to help forget, but there was nothing to keep her busy, not even letter writing. There was no one to whom she wanted to write.

The next afternoon she decided that she'd have to get out and go for a walk, just so she could be out where she could see people and try to get away from torturing thoughts. Just as she was getting ready to leave, the telephone rang.

"Where on earth have you been?" Garth's voice demanded. "I've phoned and tried to get you before I went on location and I've phoned often since I got back."

"I went home," she told him, then she related what had happened.

"I'm coming over now," he said and hung up without waiting for her answer.

He came in a few minutes and when she let him in, tears filled her eyes and she couldn't control her trembling lips. It was so good to see someone who was at least a friend, if nothing more.

He held out his arms with a smile as he closed the door and she crept into them while she sobbed quietly for a few moments, then she released herself and wiped her eyes.

"I'm sorry to be such a baby," she said, "but I can't help it. I've been so lonely and heartbroken."

"I know," he said as he drew her down beside him on the couch. "I've had my heartache too. My mother and father both died and I didn't get to see my father. He died while I was away looking for a job and I didn't know it until I went back home and found Mother alone. It isn't easy, but cheer up. You're young and time helps a lot, and you have your life before you and a future that seems to be getting brighter."

"I don't seem to care about the future," she said dismally. "It seems so little worthwhile trying to do anything but sit and mope."

"If you knew what a success your picture was, you wouldn't feel that way," he argued. "You made quite a hit, even if you didn't have the lead. I read, just the other day, a comment by some reporter. He wondered why you hadn't had more important parts. He commented especially on your voice and he predicted a great future for you. How's that? Doesn't it make you feel a little more cheerful?"

"Perhaps," and she gave him a tremulous smile.

He drew her to him and she didn't resist. She wanted to be held in his arms, to feel that here she could find release from a little of the pain that possessed her.

"Remember what I told you a long time ago?" he asked. "At least it seems a long time ago."

"You told me a lot of things," she evaded.

"You know what I mean. I told you that I loved you. You haven't forgotten?"

"No," she murmured from the depths of his arms, "but I didn't believe that you really meant it."

"Because I didn't keep on repeating it?"

"Perhaps. I thought that maybe you had changed your mind and wanted me to forget it."

"I didn't change my mind. I never could. I told you that I loved you almost from that first day, but you didn't seem to care, so I wanted to be sure of myself before I kept on repeating what I had said. I'll admit that I couldn't believe myself that it was really true. I was afraid that I might see someone else I might fall in love with, that perhaps this was just a sudden infatuation. I know now that it wasn't. It's real and I know it will last. Will you try to love me, Beth, darling? I do love you very much."

"I'll try," she said after a moment's hesitation. "Perhaps I already do, but give me a little more time. I'm so heartbroken and bewildered now that I may not really know my own feelings. I know that when I see you, my heart beats with a glad little thrill and that I want you to kiss me, but I want to be sure. If I didn't love you, marriage would be a failure and I wouldn't want it to end as so many others end in this profession that we're in. I would want it to last forever."

"I'll wait, but please don't keep me waiting too long," he said as he bent and kissed her long and clingingly.

For the first time since she had received those telegrams, her heart beat with a joy that she had thought was gone forever and she was almost persuaded to tell him now that she did love him. She wanted his nearness and the shelter of his arms, for in them she felt that life, after all, could mean something beautiful and that sorrow might fade as time passed.

"I won't," she promised, for she still wanted to be quite sure.

"Go to dinner with me this evening," he suggested. "I want to have you with me every moment possible, for I may get a call soon for another part. I have a good contract now and the time between pictures may be short."

"I'll be glad to go," she told him.

CHAPTER 19

During the next few weeks she saw Garth frequently. He was waiting for his next assignment and he was making the most of this opportunity to be with Beth.

Beth had no calls for work and she began to wonder if she ever would. Her agent was still gloomy over the loss of her part in the feature to which she had been assigned just as she went away. Her money was getting low. She didn't want to dig into what was left of her father's estate, for she knew that this wouldn't last very long and there was no one she could turn to in an emergency.

She would either get a part soon, or she would have to go out and search for some other kind of work. She wasn't qualified for anything besides her talent. She would either have to try to get a position as a salesgirl or try to get a spot in some night club. That prospect was both discouraging and humiliating. What a far cry from being a star in the musical world!

Garth had not pressed her for her answer. He didn't want to force an answer from her until she was ready to give it to him. He wondered at himself and why he had fallen so desperately in love with her. He had met so many other girls who were just as attractive as she, but none of them had stirred his heart to even a flicker.

One evening, however, after they had returned from a late dinner engagement, as he kissed her good night, he held her for a moment and whispered, "Is that little heart of yours warming up even a wee little bit toward me? I'm still hoping and waiting anxiously."

"I believe it has, more than just a wee little bit," she replied with a smile. "Just give me a little more time."

"Don't take too much time," he warned as he kissed her again. "I may have to leave again soon and I couldn't be happy if I knew I had left you here to fall in love with someone else."

"Who would there be?" she asked with a sigh. "I haven't even met anyone who might want to take your place. I'm living like a hermit, except for you."

A few days later she had a call for a bit part in an hour production. There was not much time needed for her for rehearsal in the part she was to play and it left her with a feeling of disappointment, as many of her other parts had done. She was glad to get the money, but she had no hope in this assignment of climbing to the top as a singer.

After she had finished the picture and again had time on her hands, she wondered what would happen to her as she dragged on through the years until she was finally cast aside as so many of the other young hopefuls had been cast aside when their youth and beauty had vanished. Then where would she be, without friends or parents? She'd probably end in some home for the destitute.

These gloomy and frightening thoughts were interrupted by the ringing of the telephone. It was Garth and he seemed quite excited.

"I've just received the chance of a lifetime," he told her. "In a few days I'll get a big part in a feature film to be made in Europe. Is it too late for me to come over? I want to tell you all about it. May I come?"

"Of course," she told him.

She couldn't feel at all thrilled over what he would have to say. The only thing that mattered to her was the fact that he was going away and she would be left alone once more. He wouldn't be there to make the days less dull and burdensome.

When he came he was bubbling over with excitement. He told her what the story was and of the part he was

126

to play, an important part which would give him the largest pay check that he had ever had.

She listened silently, while her heart sank lower as he related what the trip would mean and how long it would take to finish the picture.

When he had finished and she had said nothing, he looked at her in disappointment.

"You haven't congratulated me," he remarked. "Aren't you glad that I have this big chance?" he asked.

"How can I be glad when it will take you away from me for so long?" she said gloomily. "I'll be so terribly lonesome that I'll wish I could die."

"Do you really care?" he asked as he looked into her eyes while a sudden light leaped into his own. "Do you really love me? Please say yes. I want you very much, little Beth. Do you care enough to marry me? Will you marry me before I go away?"

She was silent. Suddenly, from the past there came the image of Gary and that last night when he had held her in his arms and had told her how much he loved her and how he wished that she would make it possible for him to marry her. But the past was gone forever. She had not heard from him even after the death of her parents. Surely he had ceased to care. Perhaps he had found someone else and he even might be married. She didn't stop to think that Gary didn't know her address and perhaps hadn't even heard of her tragedy.

Why shouldn't she marry Garth? He loved her and he would do all in his power to make her happy. Now that ambition had ceased to be an obsession, perhaps she could find joy in his success. Perhaps there might be a chance for her some day to use her talents in the musical world. At least she wouldn't be alone.

"If you'll marry me, perhaps I can get a part for you later on. We can be together even though I have to leave so soon. What do you say?"

"I'll marry you," she replied. "I'll try to make you happy and to be happy for you in your success."

"Do you really love me?" he asked, still doubtful.

She nodded. "Would I be marrying you if I didn't love you?"

He kissed her again, clingingly and possessively while her heart fluttered and she believed that she really loved him.

"I'll get the license and we can be married right away and then go for a few days' honeymoon before I have to leave."

She wondered if she had done the right thing or if she should have put him off a little longer. But he would be going away soon and she didn't want to be left alone.

When he returned the next afternoon he showed her the license.

"We can be married tomorrow," he told her. "We'll leave early and be married in a little town south of here, then we'll go further south for a few days. I'll be the happiest man in the world."

She was bewildered by the suddenness of it all, so much so that she couldn't think of the things she had wanted to ask him. When he had left, promising to be there early the next morning, she began to get her clothes ready for the trip.

She was ready when he came and it was not until he had put her bag in the car and they were on their way that she asked him why they couldn't be married right there in New York.

"I don't want to get it in the papers," he told her. "I don't want anyone to know that we're married. It's in my contract that I mustn't get married for at least a year. They're trying to build me up as a romantic interest and if I was already married or married within the year, that effort might fall through."

"Then what about me? Does that mean that I won't be going with you?" she asked astonished and aghast.

"Not right away," he said with a note of uncertainty in his voice. "I'll wait until I can get settled and then

128

I'll send for you. We can be together and no one need know that we're married."

"I don't like the idea," she said. "I'd rather wait until you can marry me without keeping it a secret."

"But that will take a whole year," he argued. "I don't want to wait that long. Do you?"

"No," she said reluctantly. "I hate to wait that long."

"Then please do what I ask you to. I promise that we won't be separated for long. I'll send for you as soon as I know where I'll be staying. Don't turn me down now at the last minute. We have so little time."

She agreed to go through with it, though she had her doubts about the wisdom of it. But the thought of being alone again, with him away, for she knew not how long, was more than she could face.

The town where they were to be married was not far away and he soon found the church with the parsonage next door. The ceremony was brief and they were soon on their way to a honeymoon somewhere south. They had no special destination and when he asked her if there was any place she would like to visit, she remembered the college town where Gary was teaching and she suggested that they should go through there. She explained that it was the place where she had planned to finish her education. It wasn't the truth, but he accepted what she said.

She had been thinking of Gary ever since she had promised to marry Garth. Now she felt the urge to see the place where he was working. She didn't know why she should want to see the town, for she knew that Gary was definitely out of her life and that she should forget him. It was a foolish whim, but it was what she wanted.

They rode until late that afternoon and the town was still quite some distance away and Gorth remarked that they had better start looking for a motel somewhere along the road. They usually filled up rapidly as night approached.

Finally they came to one that looked attractive, so they drove in and he engaged a room. He took their

129

bags and put them in their room, then they went out to get something to eat.

They sat there for a long time eating and talking, then as darkness fell, they went outside and sat for a while in the cool of the early night, on one of the benches outside their room.

He put his arm around her and drew her to him.

"Don't be afraid that I'll go away and leave you for long, little wife," he said. "I'll send for you, I promise, as soon as I get settled. If I could, I'd take you with me. I'll be longing for you every hour until we're together again. When we come back, I'll break the news to my director and I'll promise to keep our marriage a secret if he still demands that I do that. You won't mind that, will you?"

"Not if it will hurt your contract," she said. "I wouldn't want that to be cancelled."

She told herself that she was happy. But she couldn't help but wonder what the months and the years ahead would bring. Thoughts of Gary kept intruding upon her. She remembered the thrill that swept through her at the touch of his lips, though she knew that she shouldn't be thinking these thoughts now. She remembered the love that she had had for him, a love that was so different from this new love of the man who was now her husband. Was that old love still in her heart? She wondered. It mustn't be. It would be torment if it was.

It became late and they finally rose and, with his arm around her, they went toward their room. As they reached the threshold, he took her in his arms and carried her into the room.

"Isn't that the way it should be?" he asked playfully as he kissed her and put her down. "Happy?" he asked with his arms around her.

"Yes, of course," she replied. Just now she felt sure that she was happy, but underneath, in the depths of her consciousness, she wondered if she really would be tomorrow and the tomorrows after that.

CHAPTER 20

They had a late breakfast and they lingered at the table for a while afterward. They were not in a hurry to get anywhere. It was enough that they were together. It was enough for him that she belonged to him. He wanted to enjoy every minute with her before he had to leave her. In spite of his promise to send for her, he wasn't at all sure that he could do that. It would depend upon circumstances, where he would be housed and whether he could have her with him without letting his secret out. Much as he wanted her with him, he wasn't willing to endanger his career. He wasn't thinking of her disappointment and hurt if she would have to learn that he couldn't fulfill his promise.

Beth felt more at peace than she had since her parents had died. She now belonged to someone who loved her and whom she was sure that she loved. She was confident that her love would grow and she hoped that it would be the abiding deep love that had existed between her parents.

Though at intervals, when thoughts of the past intruded, she still felt guilty and reproached, she did not let it overwhelm her as it had done.

When they were on their way again he suggested that after they had passed through the college town, they should pick out some place that looked attractive and remain there for the rest of the brief time that they had left. She agreed to whatever he wanted to do.

As they rode toward the town where Gary taught, Beth was sorry that she had suggested passing there.

She wondered why she had had this silly desire. Why should she be interested in Gary any longer or care whether she ever saw him again? She was now Garth's wife and he should never mean anything more than a friend of the past. He should even be buried with all the other memories of the past. He must be.

The weather was perfect, and as they drove along they were enjoying every minute of the lovely scene they passed on their way.

"This is beautiful country," he remarked. "I never thought it would be like this."

"It's like every other section. Some places are lovely and then there are drab, uninteresting spots. It's beautiful where I used to live." A shade of sadness crept into her voice and a shadow passed across her face.

He saw and he changed the subject, for he knew what she was thinking and he didn't want unhappy memories to spoil their trip.

"When that picture is finished and we can settle down, we'll have to look for another apartment," he remarked. "Neither of ours will do. I want you to have the very best that I can afford," and he gave her a glance that brought a smile.

"I'll be satisfied with anything that suits you," she told him.

"That's the way an obedient wife should talk," he replied, and she laughed.

It was the first time she had laughed in a long time and somehow it helped to wipe out some of the pain that had been there for so long.

As the sun began to sink, he began to drive faster, for they were still quite a distance from their destination and he feared that they might not find a good motel.

"We may have to go to a hotel and live in style for tonight," he remarked as darkness approached.

"I like it better in a motel away from porters and bellhops and crowds staring at everyone who comes in," she said.

He didn't want to go to a hotel unless they had to. There might be just a chance that he would be recognized and that might bring on disaster. Though he was not well-known to the public as yet, there was always the chance that some keen-eyed viewer might spot him. He would either be in trouble if the news should leak out that he was married, or his reputation as a screen lover should be ruined if he was thought to be running around with some girl who wasn't his wife.

They drove along with increasing speed as darkness came and they turned off the main highway to the road that led to the town. They approached a crossroad that would have been visible in the daylight, but in the darkness it was halfhidden by tall growth along the side of the highway. Garth didn't see it. Neither did he see the car approaching along that road without lights and coming at high speed. He knew nothing until the car was almost upon him. He could neither stop his car nor avoid the crash.

The car jammed into the side where Beth was sitting. The crash broke the window of the glass that was supposed to be shatterproof and fell upon Beth as she lurched forward, striking the instrument panel.

The car swayed crazily, then righted itself as Garth continued to clutch the wheel. He was thrown against it, but managed to hold on to it, though he felt pain from the impact. He turned terrified eyes upon Beth as the car came to a stop and he saw her lying in a huddled heap on the floor of the car.

He got out of the car, for he couldn't open the door on her side and he couldn't get her out without help. He approached the terrified driver of the other car who had turned on his lights and had gotten out of the car and was standing there shocked and stunned.

"If you've killed that girl, I'll kill you!" Garth shouted, scarcely conscious of what he was saying. "Where were your headlights, you stupid fool!"

"I forgot to turn them on," the man admitted. "I was on my way to my sister's to get her to come and stay with my wife until the doctor came. My wife's having a baby ahead of time."

"Help me to get her out of there and then go and phone for an ambulance," Garth shouted. "I can't get her out by myself and I don't know how badly she's been hurt."

"I can't phone," the man told him. "Our phone is out of order."

Together they got Beth's unconscious form and laid her gently on the back seat. Then he got in and tried to start the car. It started and though it drove rather crazily, he managed to keep it on the road. He drove slowly, hoping that the car would hold until he could get help. He left the owner of the other car standing in the road wondering what he should do. Garth didn't care. It was his fault and he himself was thinking only of Beth and hoping that she was still alive.

He reached a filling station on the edge of town and was directed to a hospital not too far away.

When they lifted her out of the car, he saw that her face was covered with blood and the sight made him weak and sick. He knew that she was terribly injured even if she was still alive.

Beth was taken into the emergency room and he waited outside, fearful and trembling from shock. Even though his side hurt him terribly and he thought that he might have a broken rib, he wasn't caring about that as he walked up and down the corridor until he was forced to sit down from sheer exhaustion.

When it seemed that he would lose his mind if he had to wait a minute longer, a nurse came out and told him that the doctor would see him in a few minutes. Then she hurried away without answering his question about the extent of Beth's injuries.

After an interminable interval the doctor came out and Garth went to him, afraid to know the truth.

"How is she, doctor?" he managed to gasp.

"She's still alive," he told Garth. "For a while, we thought that she wouldn't make it, but she did. How-

134

ever, she's had a bad concussion and we can't know how bad that is until we've had some x-rays taken. Then we'll just have to wait for her reaction. If there is no brain damage, we'll have to hope for the best. She also has a broken arm. Is she your wife?" he asked.

Garth nodded. He was suddenly aware of what this would mean to his career if the truth were known, the thing that he had gone to so much trouble to keep from being known. He thought quickly, no longer in a state of shock, and decided what he would do.

"You'll have to go to the office and give a full report of the accident plus your name and address," the doctor was saying.

"May I see her before I do that?" he asked.

"Yes, but it will not make you feel any better. She's pretty well covered with bandages."

He went in and looked down at Beth lying there with a bandage on her arm and with her face almost covered with bandages. Horror took possession of him and he left the room after that one glance. The doctor looked speculatively after him as he waited in the corridor for a stretcher to remove Beth from the emergency room.

Garth told the nurse at the desk that his name was Gordon Neal and that his wife's name was Beth. He said that he lived in Holton, Alabama, and that they had been on their way north for a trip. He insisted that the accident was not only unavoidable, but that he had no idea just where it had occurred, nor did he know who it was that had hit him. He explained the circumstances and said that he was so upset over his wife's condition, that he never thought of anything else but getting her to a hospital. He said that he wouldn't try to find the man or make charges against him.

When he started back to where Beth had been, he began to feel the pain of his own injury and thought he had better see how bad it was. He was given emergency treatment by an intern who found that there was no broken rib, only a painful bruise. Then he went to the room where Beth had been taken.

He went in and sat down by the bed while a nurse hovered near. His thoughts were in chaos. In just a few days he would have to return to New York or else lose the greatest opportunity of his career. He was faced with the same decision that Beth had had to face and he was coming to the same conclusion that Beth had reached. He loved her, but he loved himself and his career more. He would stay as long as he could, then he would have to go, no matter what her condition was.

The nurse was speaking, but he scarcely heard her.

"You should be glad that there was no blod clot," she was saying. "But there is concussion, though the doctor won't know how bad it is until time passes and he can determine the result. There is no skull fracture nor depression, so in time let's hope that she will recover all of her faculties."

He was aware of only the last few words.

"What do you mean by recovering all of her faculties?" he asked dully.

Beth was already dead to him. One look at that bandaged face told him the terrible truth. If she recovered, she would be terribly scarred. She would no longer be beautiful, the lovely, fragile little person he had fallen in love with. Love had begun by the lure of her beauty and it had no depth beyond her physical appearance.

"Sometimes," the nurse replied, "after a shock like this, there is brain damage which no instrument of science can foresee. There is often loss of memory, or else the brain doesn't function normally. We hope, however, that with this patient she will recover completely. I shouldn't be telling you this, for the doctor should give you that information, but since the news seems to be good, I felt you should know it."

"Thank you," Garth said.

After a while, when Beth was still unconscious and the nurse had no idea how long she would remain in that condition, he said that he would go out and see about his car and get a place to stay for the night.

136

Late the next morning he returned. The night nurse had gone off duty and the day nurse was a stranger. He nodded to her and went to the bed and looked down at Beth. She looked even worse than she had the night before, for her face was bruised where there were no bandages and blood had oozed in little patches from under the bandages and had dried upon her skin. As he looked at her, horror took possession of him. There lay the end of his dreams of happiness. He knew that, just as surely as if Beth were already dead.

Presently the doctor came in and gave him an encouraging smile which he couldn't return.

"I'm much encouraged by her condition," he said. "I feel confident that there will be no permanent brain damage. Your wife should be able to be up and going as soon as that arm is properly set and no longer gives her too much pain."

"When will she regain consciousness?" Garth asked.

"I can't tell you that. I wish I could," the doctor replied.

"How about her face? How bad is it?" Garth questioned.

"Pretty bad, I'm afraid. Those scars will be deep and lasting. In time plastic surgery might help, but I have no assurance that it will completely restore her beauty. I'm telling you the truth, so that you won't be shocked when those bandages come off. Those cuts are pretty deep and her face may be drawn and twisted."

"Oh, my God!" Garth breathed.

"Face up to it, man," the doctor said. "She's your wife and you love her. She'll need all the love and help you can give her, for it will be much harder for her than for you."

Garth didn't reply, but stood there gazing down at the unconscious Beth.

bad because it II...[illegible]...und
on the dream ... to those reali... [illegible]
... she op ... [illegible]

CHAPTER 21

Beth's return to consciousness was so slow that the doctor began to fear that there was, after all, serious brain damage and that she might never recover, but drift into a coma. However, when he and the consulting staff had almost given up hope, consciousness began to return.

When the day nurse came in and stood by the bed watching to sec of there was any change in the patient, Beth opened her eyes and stared vacantly about her. After a moment their expression changed and the nurse realized that she was fully conscious. She stood there watching and waiting to see what would happen.

Beth turned her eyes slowly and looked at her. There was a question in them. She stared at the nurse for a few moments, then asked slowly and weakly, as if it were an effort for her to talk, "Where am I?"

"You're in the hospital, dear," the nurse told her.

Beth waited silently for a while. She seemed to be trying to remember, then she asked, "Why am I here?"

"You had a car accident and you've been asleep for a little while."

The nurse was afraid to tell her more, for she didn't know how Beth might react to it.

"You just lie quietly while I get the doctor," she advised. "He was waiting for you to wake up."

She hurried out and put in a call for the doctor.

Beth lay there trying to remember what had happened. Her thoughts were confused and she couldn't remember whether she had had a bad dream or whether something terrible had really happened. Her head ached when she tried to think and she felt so tired that she gave up the effort and closed her eyes again. This was much better than trying to think.

The doctor came in with the excited nurse. He went to the bed and spoke to Beth. She opened her eyes and looked at him. He saw with relief that her mind was clear.

"What happened to me?" she asked before he had time to say anything.

"You've had an accident and you were brought here. I'm glad that you're feeling better," he told her.

"My head hurts," Beth said. "What kind of an accident? I can't remember."

"You had a bad lick on your head. That's why it hurts. You'll remember before long."

She put up her hand to rub it across her forehead and in doing so, she felt the bandage on her face.

"What's this?" she cried, startled and suddenly afraid.

"You had a little scratch on your cheek," he told her.

That was enough for her to know now. She mustn't know the truth until she was strong enough to bear it. Pity for her filled his heart as he looked down at the side of her face which hadn't been injured. He knew how terrible the realization would be when she knew the truth.

"A little scratch with all of this bandage?" she asked doubtfully. "It's something worse than that. I can feel it. There's a drawing feeling and it hurts when I touch it. It's something horrible. My face must be all cut up." She began to cry weakly.

"Don't do that," the doctor warned, "or you'll make it worse. Your face will be all right in time, but you must get well. We don't want you to have a setback when you're getting along so well."

"When did this happen?" Beth asked as memory was struggling to return.

"Not long ago," the doctor said, not willing to tell her the whole truth.

"What day is this?" she asked.

She was beginning to realize that the horrible dream was no dream at all, but terrible reality.

He then told her the truth, for he knew that she would know it soon.

Gradually it came back to her. They were on their way to La Grange and she was sorry that they were going through there. The sight of that town would bring back memories of Gary and she wanted to forget him with the past. That was over a week from today. There was a crash and terrible pain and then there was nothing. Then at last she remembered Garth. He had been out of the picture until now.

"Where is he?" she asked. "Where is my husband?"

The nurse and the doctor cast a glance at each other. They had not believed that the couple were really married.

"He had left a little while ago," the doctor told her. "He said that he had an important business engagement and that he would be back as soon as he could. He left enough for your hospitalization for the next few days," he added.

He knew that this information might comfort her, if she should begin to worry about the bill. He saw by the expression upon her face when he told her that her husband had left, that she had something difficult to face, for he felt that the young man would not return. He was sorry that he had not reported the case to the police, but when Beth was brought in, they were too much concerned about her condition.

Beth said nothing, but closed her eyes, and they saw two tears trickle down beneath the lashes.

"I'll have something sent for you to eat," the doctor said. "Just try to eat something and don't worry, for you need to get strength to get well. I'm sure your husband will come back soon, so get well before he comes and surprise him."

"I don't want anything to eat," Beth said as the tears continued to flow. "Please leave me alone."

She lay there trying to remember all that had happened before the time when the light went out for her in the accident. Gradually it all came back, from the time she had hesitated about marrying until she had finally thought that her love was real. That first night in the motel; then their speeding toward La Grange; then blackness. She remembered that Garth had only a few days before he would have to leave for Europe with the cast. Now he had left her, wounded and unconscious, because he cared more for his ambition and his success than he did for her.

Hurt was followed by bitterness, then despair took possession of her. She had lost him. She knew that. She felt her face again and she knew the truth, even though the doctor had tried to hide it from her. She was terribly cut. She could feel the stitches drawing and she knew that she must be horribly disfigured. That was why Garth had left her. He knew that her beauty was gone. He had loved her only for her beauty. Gary would never have left her in this condition, no matter how disfigured she had been. He would have been by her side to comfort her and assure her of his love when she became aware of the terrible truth.

Why, oh why should she be thinking of Gary now when he was so lost to her? What could she do? Where could she turn? Nothing! Nowhere!

She turned her face into the pillow and sobbed until she fell asleep from exhaustion.

It was hours later when she finally wakened. There was no one there and she lay there quietly, glad that she was alone. She was trying to think clearly, what she should do, where she should go and what her life would be from now on. She knew that Garth would not return. He was gone now, she knew not where, for she had not known where he would be located for the picture. She had never thought to ask. There were so many other things to talk about.

She didn't care where he was or what he did. She

knew she could have him located through his company, but she never wanted to see him again.

Her love, which she had questioned, was now turned to hate and she despised him. She despised him for being the selfish coward that he was for deserting her at a time like this. She wished she could die, but she knew that she didn't have the courage to face eternity. She was a lost soul without pardon, but just now she had only bitterness toward God who had let this happen to her. She closed her eyes and wished that she could forget everything. Better to have no mind at all than to suffer like this.

The door opened and she shut her eyes, pretending to be asleep. She didn't want to talk to the nurse or the doctor. She didn't want to see pity in their eyes. It had been there before, but she hadn't realized why it was there. Now she knew.

Someone came to the bed and spoke her name softly and tenderly, "Beth, dear, are you asleep?"

She opened her eyes and caught her breath in astonishment while her heart skipped a beat at the sound of that voice. She saw Gary standing there looking down at her with infinite tenderness.

CHAPTER 22

It had been Gary's habit since he had been at the college, to visit the hospital as often as his time permitted. It was a missionary field near at hand, and he had had a profitable ministry in leading souls to the Lord.

The nurses knew him and always took an interest in his work. As he came in, one of the nurses greeted him and said, "There's someone in number twenty you might be able to help. She was injured in an auto accident and she's in pretty bad shape both emotionally as well as physically. Do what you can for her. She surely needs help from someone."

"I'll see her at once," Gary said, and without thinking to ask the patient's name, he went to the room and carefully opened the door. If the patient were sleeping, he didn't want to waken her.

When he saw who the patient was, he stood there so shocked that he stared at Beth for a while until he gained his composure. It was unbelievable, yet it was true. He was further shocked as he saw her bandaged face and her arm in the cast.

Pity and love engulfed him as he went to the bed and gently spoke to her.

"Gary!" she gasped, unbelieving.

Joy flowed through her for an instant until she remembered, then she uttered a little moan and turned her face away.

"Go away!" she cried. "Go away!" and tried to hide her face in the pillow.

"Is that the way to treat a friend, a friend who loves you?" he asked reproachfully.

"If you knew what's happened, and if you could see my face, you wouldn't care any more," she wailed.

"It's not your face, Beth, that's always been important to me. It's the real you whom I have loved, and was a slave to all those years. Don't turn away. I want to help you."

"No one can help me!" she cried. "Least of all, you."

She wished that she could throw herself into his arms and sob while he held her and comforted her as he had done in the past, but the longing brought only bitterness and added pain because she knew how impossible it would be.

"Tell me how it happened," he suggested. "It always helps when you talk to someone who listens with a sympathetic heart."

"Didn't they tell you at the desk?" she asked as she turned back and faced him, instinctively putting up her hand to try to hide the bandages.

"They just told me that you were injured in an accident. How did it happen? Who were you with and were they hurt too?"

How she hated to tell him the truth! How she wished that she didn't have to tell him! The words came slowly and with effort.

"I was driving with — with — my husband. He wasn't hurt."

A surprised look flashed into his eyes and she saw the pain there that he couldn't conceal.

He couldn't speak for a moment, then he asked, "He wasn't really injured?"

He knew it was a stupid question, for she had already told him that he wasn't. But he had to say something. He felt that someone had just given him a physical blow. Yet the pain he bore was worse than any mere physical blow could cause.

"No. He left here while I was still unconscious, so

144

I'm sure he wasn't. The doctor said I had a bad concussion and I was out for a long time."

"And he left you in that condition?" Gary asked. "How could he do that?"

"Because he thought more of his career than he did me," she said. "He said he would come back, so the doctor told me. He said he had an important business engagement he had to fulfill. It was important, all right. It was his big chance to get to the top in pictures. He had an important part in a picture."

Gary was silent. He didn't know what to say.

"When were you married?" he finally asked.

"A day before the accident happened. We spent one night on the way and the next day had the accident."

"I'm sure he'll come back before long," he said, trying to cheer her.

His own heart was heavy. During all the time that they had been separated, he had been hoping that in some way, if it was God's will, He would make it possible for Beth to belong to him. Now that he knew his prayer could never be answered, he was not bitter, only resigned.

"He won't come back," she asserted. "I'll never see him again and I don't want to ever see him again. He'll be gone a long time on location in Europe and by that time I'll be out of here and out of his life - - if I'm not dead. I wish I could die." Tears filled her eyes.

He took her free hand and said gently, "No, Beth, you don't wish that, for you know that you're not ready to go into eternity without Christ. Why not put your life into the Lord's hands and trust Him to take care of you and help you to bear this grief. He can give you peace."

"Peace! Peace!" she cried harshly. "How can I ever have peace with this scarred face? Don't talk to me about putting my life into God's hands. Why did He have to let this happen?"

"Think of what He has done for you in the past. He gave you a home where you were happy and where you had everything in life that you could wish for to make you happy. But you were not satisfied with what you had. You turned your back on it all, just to satisfy your ambition. God gave you a wonderful talent and if you had only given your life and your talent to Him and placed them in His keeping, there would be joy now instead of sorrow and regret and despair."

"You surely are not being very helpful," she said heatedly. "If you came here to preach to me, I wish you'd leave."

"I didn't come here to preach, Beth, but to remind you that if you still have rebellion in your heart, you should know that there can never be any peace there until that rebellion turns to repentance. I don't know why this terrible misfortune has happened to you. We both know what your mother taught you, that if you had turned your life over to God, this might never have happened. I also know that if you will let Him come into your heart even now, He can turn this tragedy into a blessing."

"I don't believe it!" she cried. "Just how do you think this could happen? What miracle could He perform to change everything that has happened to me into a blessing? How can I ever know anything but bitterness and despair, with a face like mine will always be?"

"I know this, that with God all things are possible. I'm sure that your face can be repaired with plastic surgery, for miracles were performed on soldiers who were badly scarred during the war. The most important thing is that your poor little scarred heart should be made perfect in love for God through His miracle-working power."

"How could I ever pay for what plastic surgery would cost, even if it could repair my face? That would take thousands."

"I'm sure that your husband would be willing to do that for you."

"My husband! You don't know anything of him. I do now, more than I did before. He's finished with me

146

as I am with him. He deserted me when he knew that my beauty was destroyed. He'll probably get a divorce, if he can do that without having his secret discovered. It was in his contract that he wasn't to get married for a year at least. That's one reason he skipped out so soon. I don't even have our marriage license. I don't want anything from him, not even the money for plastic surgery."

"But he should be made to take care of you, since you're his wife," Gary insisted.

"I don't want anything from him," she repeated.

"Then let me pay for the operation when it's time for it," he offered.

She turned away and began to cry pitifully. He bent over and put his arm around her. She let it remain there while she continued to cry.

"You're so kind and I've been so ungrateful," she sobbed. "I could never let you do that. Please leave me now. I'd rather be alone."

"I'll come back tomorrow, if you want me," he told her.

"Please do," she said. "You're so wonderful to me. I don't deserve anything from you."

As he rose to leave, the doctor came in. Gary waited for him in the hall. The doctor told him that perhaps the next day he would remove the bandages from Beth's face. Gary walked with him down the hall.

"She has had a narrow escape," the doctor told him. "I'm afraid of what she will do when she sees her face. It won't be a pretty sight."

"Will plastic surgery help?" Gary asked.

"I'm not sure about that. Those cuts went pretty deep, but it may do some good, even if only a little. That husband of hers deserted her when she needed him most, and he gave us a fictitious name and address. I wonder if they were really married."

"I'm sure they were," Gary told him, then he told him that he and Beth had known each other since they were children.

"She'll need someone like you," the doctor told him, "when those bandages are removed."

"How about her bill? Did her husband take care of it before he ran out on her?" Gary asked.

"Only a part. It won't cover the x-ray fees and consultations. He can be traced and made to pay all of the bill. I've never questioned her about him, though I think I should."

"She couldn't help you," Gary told him. "She doesn't know where he is and she wouldn't be any help in trying to find him. I'll take care of whatever else is owing on the bill."

"You're really a friend in need," the doctor commented.

"I don't want her to know about this," Gary said, and the doctor told him that he would do what he asked.

CHAPTER 23

After Gary had left her, Beth's heart was burdened more heavily than ever. She was burdened with the sense of frustration and regret for what she had done. There was no way out of this mire into which she had plunged herself. This knowledge filled her with even greater despair than the knowledge that her beauty had been destroyed.

When she had looked into Gary's eyes so full of tenderness and sympathy; when she had looked once more upon the face which had haunted her dreams so often, she knew that she still loved him and that perhaps she always would.

Now that it was too late, she knew that she had never really loved Garth. It was only an infatuation, born of his attentions and flattery and the love which he professed for her. Perhaps if she hadn't been so lonely, she might have realized what her real feelings were, but he offered a way of escape. She had taken it in desperation, though she knew that a happy marriage must be founded upon a love that was real and deep.

Such was the love she had for Gary. But it was too late now. She had closed the way forever. She knew that he had meant what he said, that her scarred face could not make any difference in his feeling for her, but she was now another man's wife and even if she should get a divorce, Gary wouldn't marry her. His convictions were too pronounced on that subject. She was not a Christian, and had no desire to be one.

The hurt and the burden were too deep for tears.

She lay there suffering and hopeless, wondering what she could do with her wrecked life. She wouldn't force Garth to care for her. Such a life with him would be nothing but misery.

In the midst of these torturing thoughts the doctor returned. He tried to cheer her up as much as possible, for he knew how depressed she was.

"I believe that arm can soon be carried in a sling and then you can be discharged. Doesn't that make you glad?"

"How can it?" she asked dismally. "I appreciate all you've done for me, but there's nothing that can undo what that accident did to me."

"I'm sure that something can be done," he told her. "When you're completely well and that face has healed enough, we can talk about plastic surgery. It can do a lot for you."

"How much will it cost?" she asked.

"I don't know, but it will be rather expensive. Let's not talk about that now. Just hope for the best and try to regain your strength."

When the bandages were removed from her face, the nurse uttered an involuntary gasp as she saw Beth's face. Beth heard it and she knew the worst. She asked for a mirror and the nurse, after a nod from the doctor, got one for her. Beth took one look at her face and dropped the mirror while a moan escaped her lips.

There was a jagged gash that extended from her chin to her temple, just escaping her eye, then there was another that crossed it from her mouth to her ear, a horrible cross mark upon her cheek that had once been so lovely. The stitches were still there, making the scar still more horrible.

Gary came in a little later. He hesitated as he saw the doctor and the nurse there and saw what had happened. The doctor spoke to him as he went to the door.

"See what you can do to help her," he whispered. "We can't do anything. She'll have to face the truth and live with it, at least for a while, and just now she doesn't want to."

When Gary came toward her, she hid her face under the sheet.

"Go away!" she cried. "I don't want anyone to see me. Go away!"

Gary came and leaned over the bed and said, "Beth, dear, you can't send me away. I want to help you. You must trust me."

He gently pulled the sheet from her face, and though it was like a knife thrust as he saw her terrible disfigurement, he gave no sign of the shock it was to him.

"You do have something to be thankful for," he said with a little smile. "Your eye isn't injured. You might have lost that eye. And though those cuts seem so terrible, I don't believe that any tendons were cut. Be thankful for that, for I still believe that plastic surgery can make a new woman of you."

"That's nothing to be thankful for!" she cried. "What difference if I had lost my eye? I might just as well have lost that. The doctor admitted that plastic surgery might do some good, but where could I ever get the money for it? I have so little left and I couldn't find a job anywhere with a face like this."

"Let me pay for that operation when the doctor thinks it's advisable to have it done," he begged. "Then, later on, you can pay me back, if it will make you feel better. We'll consider it a loan."

"I couldn't let you do that, for I don't know when I'd ever be able to pay you back. I'll just have to live with it. I don't even know where to go when I'm discharged from here. I could never go back to New York, even if my apartment is paid for the next six months."

"You're going home with me," he told her. "My sister is living with me and we have a nice little apartment with room enough for you. She'll come and get you and we'll try to make you happy."

"You're so good to me when I've been so mean to

151

you," she said as her voice broke. "But I can't do that. I can't impose upon you."

"You won't be imposing," he assured her. "You stay with us until you want to make some other arrangement and until you get your full strength. Maybe we can work out something. Maybe your husband will come back, after all, or you may hear from him."

"He won't come back," she asserted. "There's too much danger of having his marriage discovered. I just want to forget him."

"Then let's let the future take care of itself and in the meantime try to get well."

When he had left, she realized that there was nothing else for her to do but accept his offer. She didn't have the courage, as she told him, to go back to her apartment in New York with her scarred face.

When she was finally discharged and Gary's sister came for her, she felt secure at least for the present. She would have to do as Gary had suggested and let the future take care of what she should do.

Gary's sister, Louise, was so sympathetic and tactful that Beth was grateful and was more cheerful than she had thought she could be.

There was one thing that she did not tell Gary, and that was about her bill at the hospital. He had not paid it yet, but had told the doctor that he would do so the next day. Beth had asked for her bill and the nurse at the accountant's desk gave it to her, not knowing what the doctor and Gary had agreed upon. The amount between what Garth had left and the remainder was not large, but it frightened her, for it would almost wipe out the remaining pittance of her father's estate. However, she wrote the check and gave it to the nurse.

"That's my maiden name," she explained. "My personal account is still under that name."

The nurse said nothing, but she hoped that the check was good. When the doctor came by after Beth had gone, she told him what had happened.

He said nothing, but he knew that Gary would be surprised and also disappointed.

Louise gave Beth a little encouragement when they had reached the apartment.

"Let me help you with your hair," she suggested. "I believe I can arrange it so that you can face people without being conscious that you have a scar."

Beth consented, and after Louise had washed her thick curly hair, she arranged it in the style that many young girls were wearing. On the unmarred side of her face, she combed the hair back and held it in place with a little comb. Then on the other side, she let it hang down in soft waves that completely covered the scars.

"Now take a look at yourself," she said.

Beth looked in the mirror and a smile spread across her lips.

"Why, you've worked a miracle!" she exclaimed. "That's wonderful. I'll just remember, that when the wind begins to blow I must hold that hair down and not scare the public."

She gave Louise a hug and said, "You've been so wonderful. You've made me feel that I can go on living with a little more courage."

CHAPTER 24

Beth didn't know that the doctor suspected that Garth had given a fictitious name. She didn't tell Gary that it was nor did she mention his real name. She didn't know that the doctor had told Gary what he suspected. Beth thought it best not to tell him anything about Garth, for she didn't want Gary to try to find him. She knew that Garth would never come back nor reveal his marriage, unless he had to.

She felt that in time he would divorce her, for he would find some other beautiful face to fall in love with. She no longer felt as bitter toward him. She had contempt for him, but beyond that there was only indifference. The hurt was gone, for the love was also gone. She felt that, in a measure, she had brought this on herself, so she had no one else to blame.

Both Gary and Louise did their utmost to make Beth feel welcome and Gary, as always, was thoughtful and considerate, doing everything that he could to give her courage to go on.

She accepted their hospitality and friendship gratefully, for she knew that if they had not offered it, she would have been alone and helpless. When, however, she regained her strength and returned to the hospital for her final checkup, she felt that she couldn't stay with them indefinitely. She would have to try to find something to support herself, though she had no idea how she could do that or what she could do.

There was a more compelling reason why she felt that she must leave, besides being a burden upon them. The more she saw of Gary and the more often she was with him, the more pain this association caused. Her love for him which she had thought buried with the past, that love she was trying to forget, grew stronger. As it grew stronger, the pain in her heart also grew stronger. She felt she could no longer endure being near him, to see the light in his eyes, even though his attitude was so friendly. It made her acutely conscious of the joy that could have been hers if she hadn't thrown it away, if she had only yielded to his plea to forget ambition and to yield her life to the Lord. It was all lost to her now. She must get away where she wouldn't have to be with him so much and to bear the pain of longing whenever she was near him.

The thought of coming to God and seeking His forgiveness through Jesus Christ, was farther from her than ever. There was still bitterness over the way she had been defeated and she blamed God for letting this happen to her, though she should have known that she had no claim upon God for His protection.

Gary asked her one Sunday, when her arm was out of the sling, if she wouldn't go to church with them.

"Looking like I do?" she asked in that bitter tone. "What if the wind should blow my hair away from my face? People would turn away from me in horror."

He didn't urge her to go, for he knew that it would take time before she would have the courage to face the public. Nor did he urge her to let him pay for the operation. He thought that in time he could persuade her to let him do that. He could only hope and pray for her and for the best for her.

As she tried to think of some way that she could earn her living, even with her scarred face, she remembered one of her scenes in that last picture, where she had played and sung in a night club. Perhaps she could find a job in a night club here. She decided that she would try and see what she could do.

When Gary and Louise were both away, she took a bus and rode toward the edge of town. She saw several places that might be what she was looking for, so she got out and walked along the row of cheap eating places and night clubs. They all looked shabby and she was afraid to go in. She continued walking further and was about to turn back to catch the return bus, feeling discouraged and fearing that her idea wasn't so good after all. As she walked to the end of the block she passed one of the night club haunts and saw a sign in the window: PIANIST WANTED APPLY WITHIN.

She went in, feeling hopeful, and asked for the manager. A stout middle-aged man approached and told her he was the manager. As he surveyed her, she was thankful that her hair hid her scarred face.

"I came to apply for the position as pianist," she told him. "I saw the sign in the window. I can play and sing. I'd appreciate it if you'd try me out."

He led the way to the piano and invited her to play. She asked what kind of music he wanted and he told her what she thought he would, the latest in jazz. She began to play the same numbers she had played in her picture. Before she had finished, the few employees there stopped their work of cleaning up and listened with keen interest. When she had finished these numbers, she sang one of the other songs she had sung in her test for another picture. It was a lullaby, but it revealed her voice at its best and when she had finished, there was a round of applause from her small audience.

"Now sing something more lively," the manager said.

She obeyed and sang a familiar popular song, then turned expectantly to him, waiting for his verdict.

"You'll do," he said, "but you'll have pretty long hours."

"I don't mind that," she told him. "I can sleep all day."

He mentioned her salary, and as she hesitated, he raised the amount.

He knew that he was getting a singer and a pianist for less than he had paid his former pianist.

She accepted his offer and said she would be willing to start that same night. She was relieved that she had at last found something to do to support herself, but the irony of it all caused renewed pain. How she had fallen! From a budding starlet to a night club entertainer and in a shabby club at that. Now only the struggle for existence remained.

When she told Gary what she had done, he was both hurt and shocked.

"Please don't debase yourself by taking a position like that," he begged. "I was hoping that later on you could get a position as soloist or organist. Please don't rush into this, Beth."

"I've already signed the contract," she told him. "It's for six months. He wanted me to sign it for a year, but I wouldn't do it. All I want is enough money for that operation and, if I'm careful, I'll have almost enough to pay for it. Perhaps if my face is improved enough, I can get something better."

He said no more, but the grieved expression on his face brought pain to her heart.

She was glad that the good side of her face was turned to the audience and that the other side was in darkness. That gave her a sense of security and helped her to overcome her nervousness.

Occasionally, during the weeks that followed, someone would come up in the intervals between her numbers and try to persuade her to drink with him, but the manager quickly intervened and turned him away. She had stipulated in her contract that she wouldn't be annoyed by customers. Even in her bitterness and hopelessness, she refused to sink that low.

She managed to find a room not too far from the club and she moved there. She thanked Gary for what he had done for her and tears filled her eyes as she thanked Louise and kissed her.

She knew that she wouldn't see Gary very often and she was glad of that, though she knew that she would be longing for the sight of him every day that she was absent from him.

CHAPTER 25

Beth found life more drab and difficult as time passed. She wished that she had the courage to end it all, for she could see no future that would be different from the present. The horror of her scarred face was only one of the many things that seemed more than she could bear. There was the nightly misery of playing and singing songs that she loathed. There was also the constant effort to keep some half intoxicated fellow from slipping up to her with a whispered invitation to drink or dance with him.

The manager couldn't be present every minute, and though most of the habitues knew that she was off limits for them, they managed to try at least interest her when he was not there. She lived in constant fear that one of these insistent drunks might pull her hair away from her face and reveal that scarred side. She knew that would bring disaster.

Above everything else was the constant pain in her heart of her deep longing for Gary. This grew as time passed and she didn't see him or hear from him. She knew that he was purposely keeping from contacting her. There was no reason why he shouldn't.

She wondered how long she could keep on living like this without breaking down completely or losing her mind. Sometimes, after a particularly trying evening, she felt that she was already losing her mental balance.

When she had reached the point where she felt she couldn't go on another night, something happened that brought on a crisis. She had bought a copy of a TV magazine and she scanned through it idly. She was startled to see a picture of Garth and a write-up of his rapid rise to stardom. It mentioned his return from the picture he had finished in Europe. His picture and the article brought back memories that she had tried to forget. The article stated that the picture that Garth was to work on next, would be quite a spectacular feature.

Beth wondered if he would try to find her, but she felt that he wouldn't. She wondered what he would do if he fell in love with someone else and wanted to marry her. He would either have to have his marriage divorced, or else commit bigamy, if he didn't want to let it be known that he had been married before. Perhaps he was afraid, if she was still living, that she would try to find him and make trouble for him. She knew that he would have to make the decision, for it was his, not hers. It made no difference to her what he did. She would not be free, no matter what he did, for she could never marry Gary. That was the uppermost thought in her mind as she began to dress for her work.

That night the manager wasn't there and there was no one there to keep the habitues in check. As the evening wore on, one of them approached her as she was leaving the piano for an interval between numbers, and asked her to dance with him. There was a juke box that played dance music between her numbers.

When she refused him and told him that she was not required to mingle with the customers, he laughed drunkenly and said loud enough for everyone to hear, "What do I care about what you're not supposed to do? I want you to dance with me and nothing's gonna stop me from getting what I want. I'm gonna take you out there on that dance floor and give you a swing around. You're the prettiest little doll that's ever come into this joint and you're gonna show me how you can dance."

He put his arm around her and tried to draw her out to the dance floor. In the stuggle to free herself, her

159

hair was swept back from her face and was in the full glare of the light over the piano.

The fellow, as well as everyone else, saw the hideous scar. He let out an oath and screamed, "You're a cheat! You're as ugly as sin! Who'd want to dance with someone with a map like that?"

He gave her a shove that knocked her down. Her head hit the piano and she lay there unconscious. One of the waiters came to help her up and when he got a better view of her face, he uttered a harsh cry and stood there for a moment in shocked surprise before he tried to restore her to consciousness.

Finally Beth regained consciousness and, with the waiter's help, got to her feet. When she saw all of them staring at her and she knew what they were seeing, she stumbled from the platform and fled from the place.

With but one thought in mind, to get away from that horrible scene, she obeyed blind impulse as she fled toward the river that ran through the town. It was not a very deep stream, but the current was swift and the stream was treacherous. There had been several suicides from the bridge that crossed the narrow span.

Still following blind, unreasoning impulse, without thought of the consequence of what she was doing, she ran on until she reached the bridge. She made her way to the middle where the arch was the highest. She hesitated only a brief moment before she raised her foot and began to climb to the top rail.

As she reached the top and stood poised uncertainly before taking the plunge, she heard someone running across the bridge and a voice cried out, "Don't do that! Please stop! Don't do it! Don't do it!"

She paid no attention to the voice, and, before the man could reach her, she leaped into the turbulent water below and sank beneath the surface.

As the man reached the spot and looked about in the darkness, he couldn't see her. He knew that she had probably already been carried downstream under the bridge. He rushed to the other side and threw off his coat and slipped out of his shoes, then plunged into the water while he scanned the surface in the dim light for a sight of her. He caught a glimpse of a white skirt and he swam rapidly toward it. He managed to get hold of her and swam to the bank. He stretched her out and began to administer respiration. It took so long before she reacted to his efforts that he feared she was dead. Presently, as he continued his efforts, she began to breathe spasmodically, then more regularly.

She was still unconscious and he knew that he must get her to the hospital as soon as possible.

It was not until he took her out of the car and hastily entered the hospital, that he saw her face in the light. He had not even thought about who the girl was, for his only concern was to save her life.

When he saw her face, he gasped and uttered a prayer, "Oh, Lord, don't let her die! Please don't let her die!"

An intern came with a stretcher and Beth was taken to an emergency ward while Gary followed and waited outside to get some word of her condition. Finally the intern came out and told him that she was conscious and that he could go in.

When he went inside Beth's eyes were closed, but as he bent over her, calling her name gently, she opened them and stared at him in bewilderment.

"Gary! You again!" she gasped. "How did you know?"

"Yes, me again," he told her. "Thank God that I happened to be there when you made that jump. But I know that I didn't just happen to be there, Beth. It was God. I hadn't walked out on that bridge for months and I didn't know why I thought of going there when I did. But I was so lonely and miserable that I couldn't think straight. I thought a walk might settle my thoughts enough for me to go on with my work, so I got in my car and drove aimlessly toward the edge of town. Then I came to the bridge and I got out and thought I'd take a walk to the other side and wander through the trees in that little park. I used to go there when I first came to the college. I got to that bridge just as you reached the top of that railing. I tried to stop you, but you wouldn't listen. Why did you do it, Beth?"

Just then they came to take her to her room. The doctor thought it best for her to remain there for a while, until they could be sure that there were no complications developing.

Gary followed and waited until everyone had left her room, then he sat down by the bed and looked at her seriously.

"Don't look that way, please!" she cried. "I can't stand it."

"I look the way I feel, Beth," he replied. "Do you know what you tried to do tonight? You tried to take your life and you almost succeeded. But for the mercy of God, you would be dead now. You know as well as I what that would have meant."

His voice was not only serious, but it held a note of reproach. It sounded like her mother's when Beth had done something wrong and needed to be reproved.

"I would have sent my soul to an endless hell," she said solemnly and frankly, but she shuddered at her own words.

"Then why did you do it?" he asked in hurt tones. "If you had succeeded, you would have cut yourself off forever from those who love you and I would never see you again. My heart would break to see you go from me forever into eternal punishment."

There were tears in his eyes and in his voice and Beth began to weep silently.

"O Gary! I'm sorry!" she said brokenly. "But you don't know what happened," and she told him the whole miserable story.

"Poor little Beth," he said as he took her hand and held it. "But even that wasn't enough for you to destroy forever your hope of eternal life. God gave you

162

your life, Beth, and only God should be allowed to take back the life He gave to you and in His time. If you'll just yield your life to Him, He'll give you the strength to go on even in the face of this."

She looked at him with tears streaming from her eyes.

"Do you think that God would forgive me, or have I waited too long and it's too late?" she asked.

"Try Him and see. I know He will forgive you, if you'll only ask Him."

"I give up!" she cried. "I've been such a rebellious, selfish creature that I don't see how He can. But I'll ask Him, if you'll only pray for me. I can't go on any longer without Him. I should have asked Him long ago."

Gary knelt by the bed and poured out his heart to the Lord for her. When he had finished, she prayed. She began haltingly and uncertainly, but as she continued, the words poured from her lips between sobs. She asked God to forgive her for being so selfish and rebellious all her life and asked Him to save her poor unworthy soul.

"I'm willing to turn my miserable life over to You, Lord, and I look to You to help me to live it completely yielded to You. Help me to go on, even with this scarred face and to do what I can to atone for all of those misspent years. I ask it in the name of the Christ who died for me."

When she had finished, she greeted Gary with a smile, the first one he had seen upon her lips for such a long time.

"I believe He has forgiven me," she whispered. "Thank you for saving my life and I do thank Him for saving my soul."

He leaned over and kissed her upon her forehead.

"I'll see you in the morning," he whispered as the nurse came in.

As the door closed behind him, she closed her eyes and a flicker of a smile passed across her lips. For the first time in her life she knew peace, infinite peace, the peace that the world could not give, neither could it take away. She had faith to believe that no matter what the future held, she would have a strength that was not her own. She could face that future, because the One who had given her that abiding peace was within her and she knew that He had said, "I will never leave thee nor forsake thee."

CHAPTER 26

Gary came the next morning as he had promised. It was Saturday, and he had the whole day for himself. He was glad of that, for he was determined that Beth should not go back to the room she had occupied. He knew that it must be drab, judging from the neighborhood where it was. There were also some little details to be worked out, for he knew that since she was now a Christian, she wouldn't want to be working in that club.

Beth was expecting him. She had finished breakfast and had made herself as presentable as possible. The nurse had told her that her clothes had been taken care of. Beth knew that the nurse had done that herself and she thanked her for it. She knew that the nurse was a sincere Christian and she told her what had happened to her the night before. It was her first chance to witness for her Lord.

"I'm so glad," the nurse told her. "I knew that you needed the Lord or you wouldn't have done what you tried to do. I've been praying for you."

"My mother prayed for me for years until she died," Beth said sadly. "How I wish that I could tell her that her prayers have at last been answered."

"Perhaps she knows," the nurse offered. "The Bible says that there is joy in the presence of the angels over one sinner who repents, so perhaps that means not only the Lord, but the loved ones who are there in the presence of the angels."

"I'd like to believe that," Beth told her. "That makes me even more happy than I was."

When Gary came in and saw her bright smile and the expression in her eyes, he remarked, "I don't have to be told that something has happened to you."

"Something really has happened," she said emphatically. "I now feel that I can go on living, even with this scarred face, and that the Lord will let me use my life in some way for Him, even with this," and she put her hand on her scarred cheek.

"As soon as the doctor says you are ready for plastic surgery, we'll have that done," Gary informed her emphatically.

"Not until I can pay for it myself," she said with equal emphasis, "or have a reasonable hope of repaying you. Nothing can make me change my mind about that."

"But I'm taking you home with me today and nothing you can say can change that. You can't go back to that club," he added.

"No, I know I can't," she agreed. "I didn't sleep much last night. I was thinking of all that had happened and thanking the Lord for it all, because in the end it did lead me to Him. I'll try to find some other way to earn a living. I know the Lord will provide a way. I'm thankful for all that Mom taught me, even if I didn't yield my heart to God then. Now all those precious promises come back to me and I know that they will give me strength."

"You've learned a lot in one short night," he said with a tender smile.

"No, just remembered," she corrected.

When the doctor came, he said that Beth could leave. So Gary took her home and Louise again greeted her warmly and made her feel welcome.

Beth still hoped that she wouldn't have to stay with them long, for the same reason that made her leave before. The love she had for Gary and the pain of knowing that she could never be his wife.

Gary decided not to mention church again, for he thought he would wait until she expressed a desire to go. He didn't want to persuade her to do what he felt she should do, but she asked if she might go with them.

"I'll have to face the public anyway, so I'd better get used to it. I want to go willingly this time and not like I used to. I want to go and really worship."

Gary was delighted at her attitude. When she came down that morning as they were ready to go, she looked so lovely that he longed to take her in his arms and tell her again that he loved her. The little hat she wore was very becoming and, with her hair covering the ugly scar, no one would have known it was there.

The sermon seemed suited to her and she listened with absorbed interest, something she had never done before.

That afternoon Gary took her for a little ride, for it had been so long since she had had any diversion. They drove through the poorer section of the town on their way to the highway. As they rode down one street, they passed a little building bearing a gospel sign on the front. The sign gave Beth an inspiration.

"Oh, there is my answer!" she cried breathlessly.

"What is it?" he asked in surprise, for he hadn't seen the place nor the sign. His eye was on the road ahead.

"There is a place where I may be able to work and do something for the Lord," she told him. "I'm sure that they could use a singer or a pianist. I can at least go there and see if they can. I won't care whether they can pay me or not. I still have the money I've saved from that night club job and maybe I can help someone who was a 'down and out' as I was. I'll go there tomorrow and see if they can use me."

He offered no objections. He knew that that would be useless, and he was glad that she was really willing to at last use her talent for the Lord.

The next day Beth went to the mission. She met Mrs. Emmons, the wife of the one in charge of the mission.

When Beth told her a part of her story, and asked if she could be used, Mrs. Emmons was delighted.

"I'm sure that you came in answer to prayer," she said. "I've been trying to play and lead in the singing, but I'm such a poor pianist that I haven't had much success in keeping up the interest in the songs. We've been praying that God would send us someone. We prayed about that this very morning and here you are. How wonderful the Lord is!"

Beth told her about the accident and showed her the scar, but the sight only brought a word of sympathy.

"I believe that God can make even that bring about a blessing," she told Beth. "You can do as you did at the night club, keep that side of your face covered and I assure you that you won't be annoyed by anyone here."

She told Beth that they couldn't pay her much, but that she could have a room and have her meals with them.

"I'll be willing to work for nothing, if I can only be of service and maybe help someone to be saved from their sins," Beth told her. "I have a little money, and before that is gone, I know the Lord will supply my needs."

"I'm sure the Lord will enable us to pay you something," she assured Beth.

Beth was jubilant, and when Gary came home, she told him that she would be moving again the next day. He was glad that she was so happy, but he couldn't know what was in her heart. There was joy because of her opportunity for service, but she was also sad because, once more she would be going where she wouldn't see him very often, if at all.

"It seems that I'm always going and coming from here," she told Louise when she said good-by. "I can never thank you enough for taking me in when I needed you so much."

"You'll always be welcome," Louise assured her.

Louise knew the truth and she suspected that Beth was still in love with Gary. She felt sorry for both of them, for she loved them both.

Beth was nervous as she took her place at the piano and glanced over the number assembled there. This audience was far different from the one she had recently left and so far from the one she had dreamed of in the past. These were down-and-outers, women who had sin marked upon their faces; those who were hungry and had come for the meal that was given them, with the requirement that they should stay for the service; men who bore the marks of crime, with their hard faces and eyes that were like bits of steel looking out upon a world which they hated.

When she began to play, she forgot her audience, for her whole soul went forth in the words and the melody of her song. Mrs. Emmons had asked her if she would sing a few songs before she tried to lead them in choruses that some of them knew. As Beth sang one number, her thoughts flew back to that day when she had been so happy over the prospect of being chosen queen of the campus. She could see her mother in the doorway, unaware that Beth knew she was there. She remembered how her mother came to the piano and asked Beth to sing her favorite song, and with reluctance Beth had obeyed her mother's request. While her thoughts still dwelt upon that scene out of the past, her fingers ran idly over the keys and she began to sing "I'd Rather Have Jesus Than Anything." There were tears in her eyes and tears in her heart as she sang, oblivious of her audience, but there was a depth of reverence and worship in that song that it had never had before when she had sung it.

There was a hush in the motley audience as they listened. It was singing such as many of them had never heard before. When she finished, after a moment's silence, a woman's sobs burst forth and she stumbled down the aisle to where Mrs. Emmons was standing.

Mrs. Emmons put an arm around her as the woman

came to her and said, "That was the song my mother used to love," as her sobs interrupted her words.

She was young, perhaps not over twenty, and Beth's heart went out to her. Her own heart throbbed with agony as she heard what the young woman said.

"Let's kneel here and talk to God about it," Mrs. Emmons said as the young woman poured out a pitiful story of sin and rebellion against her mother's God.

When they had risen from their knees, while Beth played softly, she came to Beth and gave her a tearful smile. The others in the room sat silently. There were tears in many eyes.

Mrs. Emmons wasn't surprised at the unusual incident for many such miracles had happened before during the time that these faithful workers had been there. Even old habitues, sin-hardened men, looked on with sympathetic eyes.

"I want to thank you for that song," the young woman told Beth. "It was surely used of God to save my poor lost soul."

"I'm so glad that God used me to sing that song," Beth told her. "That was my mother's favorite song."

When the meeting was over, Mrs. Emmons came to Beth and put her arm around her.

"The Lord surely sent you here tonight," she said through lips that trembled. "He used you to bring that sin-hardened girl to Him. She's been here before, but has sat there skeptical and uninterested. What a wonderful talent God has given you! I never heard that song sung like that before."

Beth could scarcely talk for tears were streaming down her face.

"I never sang it like that before," she said. "That was my mother's favorite song. I never could sing it like that because I never could honestly feel what I was singing. I know that God gave me the ability to sing it that way tonight because I now can say I mean what I sing."

She was so happy that she couldn't get to sleep. She

lay there that night through long hours reviewing her life and thanking God that He had led her way He had to this moment, even though the path had gone through much suffering and hopelessness. She remembered Paul's words when he had asked the Lord to remove his thorn in the flesh and the Lord had said, "My grace is sufficient for thee." She knew that she could say what Paul had said, "Most gladly, therefore, will I rather glory in my infirmities, that the power of Christ may rest upon me."

CHAPTER 27

Now Beth understood what her mother had meant when she had tried to make her realize that there was joy in the Lord. She had closed her heart to the truth, for she didn't want to believe it. Her one desire was to have joy in the world in the way she wanted that joy and what a terrible end that joy had met!

Now she had real joy, even though she was distressed over her scarred face and though she knew that she could never belong to Gary.

There were times when she cried for joy because of a soul she had won to her Lord. She not only succeeded in making seared hearts tender and receptive again by her singing, but she had found courage to talk to the many who came to her and thanked her for her music. She had such peace in her heart that there was no room for anxiety over the future or bitterness because there seemed no financial way to have that plastic surgery performed.

At times she did feel lonely, and when her heart ached for the love which was denied her because of her own foolish mistake, she always found some passage in the Bible which her mother had put in her suitcase. She had never opened it before, but she now read it regularly. It gave her comfort and the courage to go on, no matter how hard the road ahead might be.

She was sure that Gary would find someone else as time passed. He was in constant contact with attractive young women in college and perhaps many of them were Christians. She knew that it would be a heart-breaking experience for her if this should happen, but she had faith enough to believe that God would help her bear whatever might come.

It had been weeks since she had left his home to begin this new work. She felt that this might be her mission in life. At first she thought it was only a temporary position until she could find something better, but as time passed, she began to love the work so much that she didn't even try to look for anything better. Even though the salary was small, she knew that she couldn't find anything that would satisfy her more. If this was to be her life's work, she would be content and thankful that the Lord was willing to use her after all the wasted years of selfishness and rebellion. One afternoon, when she glanced over the paper before going down to help prepare for the evening service, she found a short paragraph down in the corner of the first page.

Young actor killed on the eve of the first showing of his picture. As she read on, she was startled and shocked to see the name of the actor in question. It was Garth. The article stated that he had been fatally injured in an auto accident as he and a friend were on their way to the place where the picture was to be shown. He died not long after he was taken to the hospital.

Beth was stunned as she read the article and then she laid the paper aside. Garth was dead, and he was a lost soul. Sorrow for him and this knowledge brought sudden tears. She remembered the day when she had told him what real Christianity meant and how grave his face was as he listened. If she had only been a Christian then, perhaps he would have found salvation and the whole story would have been different. And the story of her life would have been different.

A sudden thought came to her. Now that Garth was no longer alive, she was free. That barrier had been removed. She could accept Gary's love if he offered it again. But — and she put her hand to her scarred face and shook her head. She would never burden him with such a person as she was now. She could never face his friends as his wife, when she would always be in danger of having her face seen. Gary would always feel embarrassed, though he would try not to let her know how he would feel. There was no assurance that, even if she had plastic surgery, her face would be much improved. She had her doubts about that.

She bowed her head and wept silently for a while, then she began to pray for strength to meet this situation, that even if Gary should want her, she would refuse him.

She didn't see him for several days and she was glad of that. She wondered if he had seen the item, but even if he had, he wouldn't connect it with her. He didn't know the name of the man she had married. She had never told him and, after her first refusal, he had never asked.

A few days later Mrs. Emmons called her to the telephone. It was Gary and he said that there was someone at his home who wanted to see her and that he was coming over to get her.

She dressed hurriedly and he was there in a little while. He wouldn't tell her who it was who wanted to see her. He said she would find out when she met him.

When she met the man, she thought she had seen him before, but she couldn't remember where. Gary left them together and the man told her why he had come.

"I don't know whether you remember me or not," he said, "but I was a close friend of Garth's. I suppose you know that he is dead. My name is Lawrence Field."

"I do remember you now," Beth told him.

"I was with Garth when we had that accident and with him when he died. He made me promise that I would find you and tell you how he felt about running out on you. I think his conscience bothered him so that he had difficulty doing his work on that picture. They had to make so many retakes. I think he was planning to find you and to beg your forgiveness and beg you to take him back, once this picture was finished. He said he couldn't sleep at night, thinking what a cowardly thing he had done and wishing that he could go back and undo it, if he could.

"He loved you very much, Beth," he said as he looked gravely at her.

"He had a poor way of showing it," Beth said as the words came involuntarily.

"I understand," he replied sadly. "It was cowardly and selfish of him and he admitted it with tears before he died. I can imagine how you must have felt when you knew that he had run out on you."

"I hated him at first," Beth admitted, "then I had only contempt for him. Now I know that he only did to me what I did to my parents. He loved his career more than he did me and he left me to die or get well, no matter what, just so he wouldn't lose his big chance for fame. It was a just retribution for what I did, for I ran out of my parents who had been so wonderful to me, and I forsook them when they needed me most. I was consumed by the same ambition that consumed him, so I can only feel sorry for him now that he has lost everything, even his soul."

"A lost soul?" he echoed. "I don't understand."

"We were both lost souls when we were married," she informed him, "because neither of us had come to the Lord and asked for forgiveness for our sins. Since my accident, I have learned that there is something much more important than fame. It is to have the peace of God in your heart when you know your sins are forgiven. For a time I wanted to kill myself because of my scarred face, but I've come to accept it and not to grieve over it. All I want now is to live for the Lord and to try to atone for the lost years."

"You're very courageous," he commented. "Your friend told me something about you and what had happened. I have some news for you that may make you realize how much Garth loved you and how sorry he was for treating you like he did. He left all of his money to you. There is quite a bit. He said for me to tell you that he loved you and that this might help you to forgive him for what he did to you."

"I've forgiven him already," she said with a tremor in her voice.

"As soon as the necessary arrangements can be made, I shall have the money turned over to you," he told her.

When he had left, she sat there by herself while Gary showed Lawrence Field to the door. Her thoughts were so confused that she couldn't think straight.

Presently Gary came in. He looked at her for a long moment and what she saw in his eyes caused her heart to beat as it had done in the long ago. Without saying a word, he held out his arms and she went to him and held up her lips for his kiss.

"There is so much that I could say, Beth dear, but there is no time for it now. All I want to say is that I love you and that I want your love. My arms have ached for you for so long that it was almost pain to be near you, knowing that I could never have you. Now that there are no longer any barriers, will you marry me? Do you love me enough to share my life even though there may be so little in the way of luxury that I can give you?"

"I love you enough to want you even if there would be only bread and water," she said with a smile and a light in her eyes that made his heart thrill as he held her close.

"But I can't marry you, Gary, until I've had a chance to see what plastic surgery can do for my face. I wouldn't want to be your wife and cause you embarrassment when your friends should discover what a hideous creature you have married."

"I want you to marry me now," he asserted. "I want you to know that I love you because you are you, not because of your lovely face. If the surgery is a success, I shall rejoice with you, but if it isn't, then I shall be with you to help you bear whatever may be the result.

I want you now, Beth. Marry me, please, now, not at some future time. That is too uncertain."

"If you really mean that and if you're willing to face whatever the result of that operation may be, I'd like to be married at the mission," she said. "It was there that I became reconciled to whatever God had for me and I'd like to continue to use the talent God gave me as a means to win lost souls."

"Just as you say," he agreed. "It seems to me that I've said those words before, though perhaps not in those exact words," he said, remembering the past, while a smile crossed his lips — that rare smile that she loved.

They were married at the mission. The little auditorium was packed with Gary's friends and students and with those who had been won to Christ there. Stragglers drifted in and watched the scene with curiosity and admiration as the lovely bride, with one side of her face still covered by her golden hair, murmured the words that made her Gary's wife.

Beth was seated at the piano which had been purchased recently. She let her fingers run idly over the keys, then she began to play the song that her mother had loved so much and she softly hummed the words. Memory brought pain as she thought again of that day when her mother had stood in the doorway listening to her. It also brought joy, for she was walking in the way that her mother had prayed for, for so many years. She could now sing that song with her whole heart, for she believed every word of it.

As it had happened on that day, today someone slipped into the room and put his arms around her. She turned and gave Gary a smile and rested for a moment in his arms. Her hair was cut shorter now. On one side of her face there was a dim white line where a hideous scar had been. She said it was a little memento of what Garth had done to try to atone for his selfishness and cowardice.

"Are you happy, my darling?" Gary asked as he held her close.

"What a silly question!" she exclaimed. "With a husband like you and a face that's no longer hideous, and a God whom we both love and want to serve together, a God who loves us and has redeemed us, what more could I ask for?"

"Nothing, my darling, nothing," he replied as his lips met hers.